SUDDEN MAIL-ORDER BRIDE

REGINA SCOTT

*To my mother and father, who met at the
Evergreen Ballroom, not far from Hawks Prairie,
and who tiptoed around a proposal, and to the Lord,
who offers His love to all.*

CHAPTER ONE

Near Olympia, Washington Territory
Late March 1877

IF SHE HAD to marry a stranger, she'd picked a pretty place to do it.

Caroline Cadhill peered out from the bed of the wagon that was bumping along a muddy road in the middle of nowhere. After leaving Olympia, she'd lost all sense of direction. The sun was masked by puffy white clouds, so she couldn't even be sure of the shadows. But she was fairly certain those larger white things on the horizon weren't clouds. They were mountains.

Real, snowy mountains.

She shivered, but more from excitement. *Ready or not, Jeremy Willets, here I come!*

The postmaster in Olympia had recommended this farmer to take her the last leg of her long journey. Now he called to his horses and drew them to a stop beside a drive that opened to the right of her. "Here you go, miss. This is where the Willetses live."

He made no move to help her down, but she was used to such things now. Ever since Father had been convicted of a crime she still couldn't believe he'd committed, everyone she'd known in Cincinnati had kept their distance, as if she'd contracted consumption. And on the way West, most folks had been too focused on their own affairs to pay a stranger much mind.

So, she scooted to the open end of the buckboard, dragging her valise with her. "Thank you very much for the ride, Mr. Abercromby. I hope to see you again."

He grunted. Likely he wondered whether she was going to be staying more than a few minutes.

She wondered the same.

She shinnied off the end of the wagon, then arranged her gray coat and gingham skirts about her. She'd barely had time to lower the bag before he clucked to the horses and rattled off down the road. Straightening her bonnet, she picked up the battered leather valise and started up the drive.

All around her, grasses bright with the green of spring waved in a cool breeze. Roan cattle raised their heads, chewing contentedly, to watch her pass. To their backs stood the solid, dusky green of a forest, its depths shadowed and mysterious. The air smelled clean, as if freshly washed.

You're a long way from home, Caroline.

And wasn't that the point? No more pretending that she hadn't lost everything and being pitied and shunned anyway. No more living along a dusty street where men shambled about begging for a penny for bread. No more fearing she might not have enough money for bread for her and Ned.

The thought of her brother was like a storm cloud darkening the sky. Why had he left without telling her? Where was he now? Was he safe? Fed?

Please, Lord, keep Your hand on him and give me strength to follow this path.

Ahead, a white clapboard two-story house came into view, twin barns rising behind it. A wide porch crossed the front, with chairs here and there under the windows as if to encourage lingering with a book and a cup of tea.

The two young red-headed women in the yard seemed far more industrious than the porch implied. Aprons covering much of their gingham dresses, they were hanging clothes on a line that stretched from one porch pole to a pole in the middle of the yard.

Jane? Jenny? Joanna? Joy would surely be smaller. Caroline's steps quickened.

"I have a large family," Jeremy Willets had written to her after she'd emboldened herself to answer his ad for a mail-order bride. "Four sisters and five brothers, although the oldest brother lives north of us quite a distance. There may not be a town near the ranch, but we've never lacked for good society."

That was one of the things she'd admired about Jeremy. He knew how to turn a phrase. And over the course of the next three months, as they'd corresponded, she'd learned all about his siblings, from their ages and descriptions to their personalities. She'd thought she'd also learned something of the man in the process.

He preferred to find the laughter in trouble instead of hanging onto the pain. She had the same philosophy. He looked for the easiest, quickest ways of doing things, which she had to remind herself to do.

"Some might call that laziness," he'd written. "I see it more as efficiency. You could spend hours tilling, planting, and harvesting your own hay for the winter feeding of the stock, but why not buy some from the farmer down the road, who will thank you for helping his family?"

And that came through most of all: Jeremy Willets cared deeply about family. He might tease and joke about his, but it was clear he'd do just about anything for them. She suspected that was the reason he hadn't sent for her yet. He wasn't convinced she would fit.

She hadn't truly fit in Cincinnati. As the daughter of a bank clerk, she wasn't wealthy enough to be considered a member of high society but too wealthy to be accepted in lesser society. Her father had paid for her to attend a girls' school as a day student, but she'd been the only one who had to hurry home from lessons to tend the house. She was used to being the oddity.

At the moment, she had higher hopes for finding somewhere safe to stay for a while. Surely he'd agree to that, even if he had decided not to marry her.

The taller young lady noticed her first, and my, was she tall! Caroline would have put her at least six inches above her own five-and-a-half-foot height. She had managed to tame her hair back into a bun at the nape of her neck, but that couldn't hide its fiery nature. She had to be Jane, the oldest of Jeremy's sisters.

The other young lady must have seen her sister start, for she turned to eye Caroline as well. Her hair was sleeker, her blue gaze surprisingly warm.

"Only Jenny has blue eyes." She heard Jeremy in her head, at least, what she'd come to think of as Jeremy's voice from his letters. "No one is sure how that happened, as the rest of us have either brown, gray, or green eyes."

"Can we help you?" Jenny asked.

Caroline lugged the valise closer. "I hope so. I was told this is the Willetses' ranch."

A third girl came skipping around the house just then, only to pull up short, her copper-colored curls bouncing to a stop. "No, it's not," she said as if she'd heard Caroline.

Caroline's stomach shriveled.

"Joy," Jane said in a warning.

"It isn't," she told her two sisters. "Jack said I could name it. I decided on the Jumping J."

Caroline couldn't help her grin. "Because you all have names starting with J! Perfect!"

Now they all stared at her.

"Who are you?" Jane asked, putting herself in front of the others as if to protect them.

Oh, could she have introduced herself any more poorly? She stuck out her free hand. "Miss Caroline Cadhill. Your brother Jeremy likely mentioned me."

The three exchanged glances, and her hand fell with her hopes. Surely he'd talked about his courtship with his family. Had something happened to him since she'd received his last letter three weeks ago? Perhaps they'd written to her in Cincinnati, not knowing she was heading their way.

The front door of the house opened, and a brown-haired older woman with a round face and ample frame came out onto the porch. About to shake a rag, she paused.

"Girls! You never told me we had company!"

His mother. It had to be. Caroline smiled at her, praying for recognition, acceptance.

"This is Miss Cadhill, Ma," Jane said, never taking her gaze off Caroline. "She says she's acquainted with Jeremy."

"Well, friends and acquaintances are always welcome," their mother replied. She tucked the rag into the pocket of her apron and motioned to Caroline. "Come on in now. Jane, see about refreshments. Jenny, fetch your Pa. Joy, go find your brother."

As if long used to being directed, the three sisters headed off.

Still not sure of her welcome, Caroline climbed the steps onto the porch and followed Mrs. Willets into the house. A hallway stretched from front to back along a staircase leading up. The room at the right appeared to be the dining room, with a large table and more chairs than she could count quickly. The walls were whitewashed, but the strawberry gingham curtains were bright and cheerful.

"How do you know my Jeremy?" his mother asked as

she led her into the parlor on the left and took a seat on the brown horsehair sofa by the rounded-stone hearth.

Caroline set down her valise. "I'm his mail-order bride."

Mrs. Willets blinked, then shook her head. "That boy. Is this another of his jokes?"

Jokes? *No, please, Lord, no!*

"I don't think so," Caroline managed. She nearly collapsed onto the nearest ladder-back chair. "He's been writing to me for months."

Somewhere, a door slammed, and footsteps thudded closer. A minute more, and a man stood framed in the doorway. He was tall, with the breadth of shoulders and length of legs the girls at Miss Wilmont's Academy tended to moon over. His hair was thick and as deep a red as the cattle he tended, and his green eyes caught the light from the window like the emerald ring that had been her mother's. The look he directed at Caroline could only be called charming. Why, he was nearly as handsome as the view. Were her circumstances turning at last?

"You wanted me, Ma?" he asked in a voice that sounded very much like the one in her head.

"Jeremy," his mother said sternly, "I have just been introduced to your mail-order bride. What have you done?"

Jeremy Willets gaped at the woman who had appeared in the parlor like a bolt out of the blue. Caroline Cadhill was supposed to be in Cincinnati, more than two thousand miles away. Yet he couldn't deny this lady looked much as Caroline had described herself in her letters.

"I'm not too tall," she'd written in one of their early correspondences. "My brother, Ned, is about six feet, and the top of my head comes just under his nose. He complains there's not enough meat on my bones, but I find it sufficient to keep me strong. At least, I've never been mistaken for a boy. My hair is the color of coal, and it has a few curls in it naturally. My eyes are brown."

Brown and big and staring back as if he were her last hope.

"Caroline?" he asked.

A smile blossomed, transforming her narrow face and tugging at something inside him. "I *knew* you couldn't be teasing. Yes, it's me. I came to find you."

The scowl on his mother's face was sharp enough to nip the bud of delight at meeting Caroline at last. That reaction was precisely why he hadn't sent for her yet. He and his family didn't always see eye to eye, and never more so than in the matter of love and marriage. Ma and Pa had taught them all to believe in, nay, extoll, the virtues of true love, starting at first sight.

He had never been able to convince them that not everyone was cut out to find such a love, especially in a territory where men outnumbered women eight to one.

But none of that was Caroline's fault. She had come a far piece and on her own funding. A young lady alone. She had spunk, but he'd never doubted that, not after her letters.

He stepped into the room. "Well, how nice to finally meet you face to face."

"Yes," Ma put in before Caroline could respond. "It would have been nice if we had had any idea she was coming."

He loved his mother. Truly. But she was a force of nature. Best to calm the storm now. But before he could smooth things over, Caroline jumped in.

"I'm truly sorry about that, Mrs. Willets," she said, voice contrite. "Things took a turn for the worse back home, and the only thing I could think of was to head West. Two trains, a steamer, and a couple of wagon rides later, and here I am."

Her smile was so pleased that even his mother relented. "Well, you have traveled far. Why don't you rest a spell? I'll just help Jane with those refreshments." She rose and affixed him with a glare. "Jeremy, I'll need your assistance as well."

"Right behind you," Jeremy promised as she swept past him into the hallway. He darted to Caroline's side. "Proud of you for getting here all on your own. That took courage. Sorry if the welcome didn't live up to expectations. We can be a cantankerous bunch."

She angled her head as if to spy his mother out the door. "I hope I didn't cause any difficulty."

"Nothing we can't handle," he assured her.

"Jeremy Dalton Willets!"

He grimaced. Just what every man wanted, to be scolded by his mother in front of the woman he intended to wed. With an apologetic look to Caroline, he strode out the door.

His mother was waiting only far enough from the parlor door that they might not be overheard. "A mail-order bride!" she sputtered. "What were you thinking?"

"I was thinking that a man who's reached nine and twenty years of age ought to be able to manage his own courtship," he said, keeping his tone light and look endearing.

His mother drew in a breath. "I had hoped so as well. Fine. Go talk to your bride then. We'll be along shortly." She headed for the end of the corridor and the door to the kitchen.

Shoulders feeling unaccountably tight in his work shirt, Jeremy returned to the parlor. Caroline was perched on the edge of the chair, as if expecting to have to flee at any moment. Or maybe she thought his mother would yank the chair out from under her.

He went to take the seat closest to hers. "I'm glad you came."

Her eyes widened. Brown could be a rather drab color, but her eyes swirled with green and gold as well. In fact, he had a hard time pulling his gaze away.

"You are?" she asked.

"Yes, despite the welcome or lack thereof you received from my family," he told her. "I'm only sorry you had to come all this way with no help."

She shrugged, the movement raising the loose gray wool coat that covered much of her plain blue gingham dress. His sisters begged for flounces or a bit of lace. She didn't seem to have any.

"It was fine," she said. "You wouldn't believe all the sights you can see. At night, the whole sky lights up with stars!"

He nearly winced at the idea that she'd had to sit up all night, yet he couldn't help but admire her ability to look on the bright side. That was one of the things he'd liked about her letters.

"I would have been happy to pay for a first-class ticket so you could have had a berth," he said. "And I could have met you in Olympia or Puget City."

She peered up at him shyly, thick black lashes fluttering. "That would have been nice. But I didn't want to put you to any trouble."

He glanced out the door. "Oh, I can get into trouble well enough on my own, but thanks."

She flinched. "I'm sorry. I thought they'd know about me."

They would have known if he'd have screwed his courage to the sticking point and told them. But he'd had plenty of time. He and Caroline were only corresponding. No one had proposed or accepted yet. He could ease the idea into conversation with his family, prepare them for a bride they didn't know.

A marriage built more on companionship to start than love.

She kept gazing at him, eyes moving from his hair to his chin to his clothes. At least he'd shaved that morning. Sometimes after a night in the saddle, he didn't bother. A shame he hadn't dressed in his church clothes, but he'd hardly expected to meet his bride. At least the flannel shirt and twill trousers were practical and fairly clean.

But the more she looked, as if studying his very soul, the more he felt like squirming.

Not her too, Lord. Are You the only one who can appreciate me for who I am?

He found himself leaning back in the chair to escape the scrutiny and forced himself to relax. "I probably should have told them sooner," he admitted, "but I wasn't sure we'd suit."

It was only the truth. Still, she might have taken umbrage. If she'd been willing to travel so far, she must have been a lot more sure than he had been.

She merely nodded. "I know. We hadn't made that decision yet. And I'm sorry to arrive all of a sudden like this. But I was in trouble, and I didn't know where else to turn."

Jeremy stiffened. "Trouble? What kind of trouble?"

She visibly swallowed. "The worst kind of trouble. Men came to the lodging house, threatening to hurt me if I didn't tell them where my brother had gone. I don't know where Ned is. He ran away a month ago, after Father was put in prison. I've been trying to manage on my own, but I just didn't feel safe anymore. Please, Jeremy, can I count on you to protect me?"

He could feel her fear, her worry. Something warned him he ought to feel as worried for his family. Had he brought danger to their door?

But all he wanted to do was pull her close, comfort her.

A shame they were about to have an audience.

He contented himself with pressing his hand over hers as it rested on her skirts.

"You're safe here, Caroline," he said. "You can stay for as long as need be."

Even if that meant he'd have to come to terms with his sudden mail-order bride.

CHAPTER TWO

WHY HADN'T HE told her he was so handsome? The light in those deep-set green eyes was as compelling as the forest edging the ranch. And when those firm lips turned up in a smile, she felt all tingly inside, as if Christmas had come early.

Then again, men probably didn't think to mention their looks, although they certainly considered a woman's looks before deciding on a courtship. They considered her dowry and family connections too. At least, those were the reasons her father had insisted none of the young men of their acquaintance had been interested in being more than friends.

"You're clever and kind," he'd say, standing over the sink and scrubbing the ink stains off his cuffs. "And you have a good heart. That will count for something with the right man."

Somehow, she'd reached the age of three and twenty, and the right man hadn't come knocking at the door. So, she'd emboldened herself to purchase one of the newspapers in which frontier gentlemen advertised for brides. Her correspondence with Jeremy Willets had made her hope that they would be comfortable together.

But gazing at him now, all muscle and bright eyes and smile that tugged at her heart, she wasn't nearly so sure.

Would someone like Jeremy Willets really want to marry her?

He'd said he'd protect her. That was the most important thing, and she was thankful. She shouldn't get her hopes up for more.

"Let me take your coat," he said now, rising.

Caroline rose as well. She started pulling on the sleeves, but he came around behind her and lifted the wool smoothly from her shoulders, as if they were an old married couple and had been tending to each other's needs for decades. His fingers brushed her neck, soft as a caress, and that tingle grew.

"So your father was convicted?" he asked, draping the coat over her chair as if he thought she'd need it again shortly. "The last letter I had from you, he had just been arrested."

That had been a very difficult letter to write, but she'd felt it only fair that he know. Her father might be innocent of the crimes that had landed him in prison, but the scandal of the trial had tainted the entire family.

"A lot has happened since I wrote you," she explained, returning to her seat. "My father is in prison while his lawyer attempts to appeal. And Ned disappeared with no explanation. I left Cincinnati two weeks ago, so if you wrote back, I didn't get it." A thought popped into her head, and she stiffened. "You didn't stop writing, did you? Had you decided we wouldn't suit?"

"No, I…" he started, but footsteps heralded the arrival of his mother and two sisters. Joy wore a big smile. Jane wore a frown, but at least she carried a plate of cookies.

"Ma says you're going to marry Jeremy," his littlest sister said, plopping down on the chair on the other side of Caroline and gazing at her with eyes a storm cloud gray at odds with her sunny personality.

Caroline's cheeks heated. "We're still talking about that."

Joy's brow puckered. "Why?"

"Because that's what folks do when they're courting," her mother said, setting down a tray with a pitcher of lemonade and glasses on a nearby side table. "Jeremy, introduce Miss Cadhill to your sisters."

"Caroline," he said obligingly, "this is my oldest sister, Jane, and my youngest, Joy."

Jane inclined her head as she held out the platter for Caroline to take a cookie that smelled of ginger.

Joy hopped to her feet and spread her skirts in a curtsey. "Very pleased to make your acquaintance, I'm sure."

Their mother smiled her approval as more voices sounded from the hallway. In a matter of moments, the parlor filled with Willetses: his father, three of his brothers, and another sister. Jeremy introduced her to them while his mother handed her a glass of lemonade.

Caroline nodded, clinging to the cool glass with one hand and the soft, warm cookie with the other as she recalled what Jeremy had written about them.

The tall, burly fellow with the flaming hair was his older brother Jack. He acted as ranch foreman.

Jason and Joshua were the youngest boys, on the edge of adulthood, jostling each other for position. Joshua's hair was a deeper red than his brother's, but they both had brown eyes.

Joanna's hair was curly, like Joy's, though Joanna's was almost brown, and her gray eyes were brighter, like silver. When she grinned, it was impossible not to grin back.

Caroline enjoyed every moment in matching names to faces and descriptions, but perhaps she looked dazed, because his mother rose and flapped her hands. "That's enough for now. You can all become better acquainted over dinner. We'll see you then."

The clump of boots and the clack of heels disappeared down the corridor, and doors closed in the distance, leaving her and Jeremy alone with his mother and father.

Caroline munched on the cookie a moment in the silence that fell. She tasted another spice under the ginger—nutmeg? Perhaps she'd have a chance to ask.

"How do we come to find such a lovely young lady in our parlor?" Jeremy's father asked with a kind look her way. He couldn't have been more different from her father, who was small, slender, and stoop-backed from bending over his ledgers all day. Mr. Willets was tall and well built, leaning back on the sofa as if comfortable with his place in the world. It was clear where everyone's red hair had come from, even if his was beginning to gray at the temples.

Mrs. Willets looked to Jeremy. "Exactly what I'd like to know. We taught you better than this, Jeremy Willets."

Caroline would have wilted under the tone if anyone had used it with her. She hastily downed a slug of lemonade.

Jeremy merely set aside his glass and smiled at his parents. "You and Pa taught me very well, Ma. And I will always be grateful. But you claim to have fallen for each other at first sight, as if God put a big red sign on your foreheads saying, 'This is the one.'"

Caroline gaped at them. "Love at first sight! How marvelous!"

Jeremy raised his brows even as his mother raised her chin.

"It *was* marvelous," she insisted. "And that's the sort of love I want for all my children."

"A very noble goal," Caroline assured her.

"But not everyone gets that kind of love," Jeremy was quick to point out. "Look at Jesse and Alice. They wed after being forced to spend the night together in a storm." Jesse was the oldest of the sons. Jeremy had written to her about how his brother and his bride were now very happy together.

"But love grew," his mother protested. "They just had to try harder than some."

"And what makes you think love can't grow between me and Caroline?" Jeremy asked. He reached for her hand and held on tight, as if he'd never let go.

Caroline stared at their entwined fingers, then up at him. Did he truly hope for a love between them, a love like his parents had? Her own hope rekindled until she was sure it was shining from her eyes, her face. She'd come all this way with the idea of seeking safety and had been prepared to wed for convenience. Wouldn't it be simply wonderful if Jeremy Willets came to love her instead?

He'd thought he'd have to fight, but he hadn't been prepared for Ma to marshal her arguments and demand true love from the start. He'd mistaken the emotion once before. He didn't intend to fool himself again.

"Love can grow, son," his father said, "if you and Miss Cadhill are certain you have enough in common." That was Pa, always the peacemaker. Jesse had learned it at his knee, and everyone else had benefitted from it. Jeremy nodded his thanks for the support now.

"Caroline and I have written to each other for months," he told both his parents. "I can reasonably say I know all about her."

For some reason, that made Caroline drop her gaze and fiddle with her skirts.

"Well, that's real nice," his father said, giving his mother a look as if to encourage her to agree.

"What people write and what they do are not always the same," she said primly. "You likely need more time together to know your own minds."

Jeremy tried for charm, giving her his best smile. "Why, Ma, you always said I knew my mind entirely too well."

"And can your Caroline say the same?" she challenged.

"Well, I…" Caroline started, gaze coming up to his. Was that doubt in the depths of the brown? His spirits sank, and his grip on her hand tightened as if some part of him thought she'd be ripped away at any moment.

His mother pointed a finger at his chest, as dangerous as a loaded revolver. "You see? You can't rush a woman to the altar, Jeremy! No good will come of it. I expect you two to enter into a proper courtship."

Caroline bit her lip. Proper courtships generally meant the gentleman living in one house and the lady in another. Her house was thousands of miles away. And she wouldn't have funds for lodging here, even if Puget City had held a hotel or rooming house where he'd feel comfortable leaving her.

"I promised Caroline she could stay here," he told his mother. "Knowing how you feel about hospitality, I'm sure you'll agree."

"Of course Caroline can stay here," his mother said. "She can sleep in your room. You and Jacob can move in with Jason and Joshua."

Four of them in a room built for two? His brothers weren't going to thank him for that. But at least she wasn't going to order Caroline out of the house. He'd take that concession as a victory.

"Maybe I can bunk with Jack over the barn," he suggested. His oldest brother had been given his own quarters in deference to his seniority. That and the fact that he was the most likely to butt heads like a goat with the others. The rooms had been Pa's idea. Of course.

"Perhaps I should be the one to stay in the barn," Caroline offered. "Hay can be very comfortable, I hear."

She was easing the way. Jeremy was ready to protest, but even his mother would have none of it.

"Nonsense," she said. "You're a guest in this house. Jeremy, go clear out your things and your brother's. Caroline can stay here with us until the room is ready."

Leave her to his mother's questionable graces? Not on his life.

Pa must have had similar concerns, for he put his hand back on Ma's shoulder. "Perhaps Caroline would like to rest. We can be a bit much." He winked at Caroline, and she smiled. The tightness in Jeremy's chest loosened.

He stood and held out his hand to her. "I have a better idea. The best way to get to know each other is to spend time together. You said so yourself, Ma. Caroline can help me clear out the room. We'll leave the door open, and you can come check on us at any time." Their busy household didn't hold much privacy as it was.

Caroline put her hand in his. Such a tiny hand, soft and fragile. He wanted to cradle it close.

"I'd be happy to help," she said.

He took her valise with his free hand, and she pulled her coat from the chair. Then he led her out the parlor door before his mother could protest.

"I'll send Joy up to act as chaperone!" she threatened from behind him.

Jeremy didn't respond. He could manage his littlest sister.

"Are you all right?" he asked as he led Caroline up the stairs for the top story of the house. The second floor was divided into four rooms, two front and two back. His sisters had the north side rooms, and he and his brothers had the south side.

"Your mother is very angry with us," she murmured with a glance back toward the parlor door.

"My mother is very angry with *me*," he told her, opening the door at the top of the stairs on the right. "I've heard worse."

He ushered her into the room he shared with Jacob. A bed stood on either side of the dormer window, the colorful quilts and wool blankets neatly tucked in as Ma insisted. Pa had built the bedsteads along with the wardrobe and highboy dresser against the wall on their right. It was all plain and simple, but it was home.

He'd slept in this room, in that bed, since he was nine, and his father had finished the house after they'd lived first in a tent and then in a single-room log cabin.

But Caroline looked around, wide-eyed, as if she'd never seen anything finer. More likely she had seen many things finer and was wondering how he made do with such a small space.

"You never had to share a room," he guessed, bending to smooth the quilt.

"Ned and I had our own rooms," she said. "But I always wanted a sister to share with. You're blessed to have so many!"

He chuckled, straightening. "It feels like a blessing, most days. But don't get on Jane's bad side. She has a vocabulary, and she isn't afraid to use it."

She glanced toward the door again. "They all seem so friendly. Do you think they'll like me?"

It was a question that every bride must ask about her new family, but her voice sounded plaintive, as if she was certain he'd tell her no.

Jeremy went to take her hand and give it a squeeze. "None of my brothers and sisters lack for intelligence. So, of course, they'll like you."

She beamed at him. When she pulled her hand from his, he felt as if he'd lost something precious.

"Where are your brother's things?" she asked. "I can gather those while you gather yours."

Jeremy roused himself. They had a purpose for being up here, besides this ridiculous courtship Ma was insisting on. Maybe Pa would talk her out of that before dinner.

Though he didn't hold out much hope. Once Ma made up her mind, little changed it.

"Start in the wardrobe," he advised. "The charcoal-colored suit, white dress shirt, and black shoes are Jacob's church clothes. The second drawer in the dresser has his, um…" A lady shouldn't have to deal with his brother's underthings, or his.

"I'll take the dresser," he decided. "You just gather everything in the wardrobe."

She went to work, but she kept eyeing him, as if she thought he'd run out on her. It sounded as if many in her life had left her, even if they'd had no choice. Her mother had died when Caroline was a girl, and Caroline had helped raise her little brother, who was only a year or two younger. Now it seemed Ned was gone, and her father was in jail.

"How's your pa doing?" he asked. "It can't be easy for a gentleman to be sent to prison, especially knowing himself innocent."

"I'm very proud of the way he's persevering," she said, carefully folding his brother's shirt. "I told Mr. Marchand, the manager at Cincinnati Savings and Trust, that Father couldn't have done what they said. He promised he would look at the audit again but that he didn't think leniency was called for with such a large amount of money missing."

"Where did it go?" Joy asked, flouncing into the room and throwing herself down on Jacob's bed. She gazed at Caroline expectantly, as if the story was fiction and not the facts of Caroline's life.

Caroline straightened and licked her lips. They were full and rosy, and they likely felt as soft as they looked. He was so busy staring that he almost missed her answer.

"No one knows, Joy. The trustees of the bank blamed my father for embezzlement and held him up on charges. They claimed he'd been siphoning off money and giving it to people who needed it, but they only found one witness who said he'd seen my father doing it. So, my father was convicted and sent to prison, and the bank took everything we had to recoup their loss."

How could she say that with such a sunny smile? His heart would be breaking. It broke just listening to her.

"Maybe he hid the money," Joy said. "Maybe he knew the bank would use it for wicked purposes."

Caroline wrinkled her nose as she folded Jacob's coat as well. "Cincinnati Savings and Trust mostly helps families and their businesses. I don't think they've done anything wicked or illegal, except for insisting my father was a criminal. For all I know, at some point, they'll discover it was just a clerical error."

There she went again, trying to make a tragedy less tragic. All he could see was that her father, her brother, and even the bank manager had failed her.

Did he have it in him to be the hero she needed, or would she turn away from him like the last woman he'd thought he'd loved?

CHAPTER THREE

T HEY FINISHED MOVING Jeremy's and his brother's things to the other room in time to come downstairs for dinner. The sound of voices greeted Caroline before she even stepped into the room.

After their mother's death, it had been just her and Ned. Their father might join them for dinner, but, more often than not, he worked late or brought ledgers home with him. She'd told herself he was just being conscientious, but some at the bank had insisted that this had been his opportunity to change the numbers in the books to hide his misdeeds.

Her father might have been overly generous in his donations to help those in need, but he would not have stolen money to support others. She hadn't been allowed in the courtroom, but Ned had reported the evidence of his guilt was spotty at best. Still, money was missing, and the most likely suspect was her father. Someone else must have been involved, but who? The riddle had gone around and around in her mind as she'd traveled West, and it still made her head spin.

So did trying to keep up with Jeremy's family.

His father was standing at the head of the table, hands braced on the back of the hardwood chair as Jeremy led her and Joy in. His brothers and sisters were filling in the sides, and there seemed to be some confusion as to the seating arrangements, because they kept bumping into each other and looking at their mother as they moved about.

In the end, Caroline found herself seated next to Mrs. Willets near the foot of the table. At least Jeremy was beside her. She wasn't sure what was expected of her, but she was beginning to realize she could count on him to intervene if anything became too trying.

His father said the blessing, and everyone began passing dishes around: a porcelain tureen of stew, a pewter platter with squares of cornbread, and a bowl of something purple, shiny, and lumpy. Would they think her a glutton if she loaded her plate?

"Serve your sweetheart, Jeremy," his mother directed as he started to pass her the tureen.

"I hardly think we all want a taste of Caroline, Mother," he said with a wink to Caroline. "And I'm not sure Joy could lift her to pass her on to Jane."

Joy giggled at his silliness, but his mother shook her head.

He bent closer to Caroline. "I suppose I should be a gentleman and spoon you up portions, but I have a feeling you know better than I do what you'd prefer."

"All of it," she told him. "It looks delicious."

His brows went up as if impressed, and he proceeded to fill her plate.

Some girls at the academy had picked at their food, claiming that eating little made them appear daintier, more refined. His mother and sisters seemed to be eating heartily, so Caroline did too.

Oh, how nice to have butter for the cornbread again! To sink her teeth into the stew meat and not have to chew for minutes to get through the tough parts. The lumpy material turned out to be a berry preserve, but she didn't recognize the type. It was sweet and tangy at the same time. She was enjoying every bite when the questions started.

"Where are you from, Miss Cadhill?" his mother asked as she spooned up another mouthful of stew.

Caroline hastily swallowed. "Cincinnati, ma'am. Near the foot of Mount Adams, until recently."

She wasn't sure if the burgeoning neighborhood would mean anything to his family, but she might as well impress as much as she could.

His mother seized on the last word instead. "Recently? Had you moved?"

"Caroline moved out of her father's home to a lodging house," Jeremy put in smoothly. "And I, for one, commend her for her courage and fortitude."

Jane lifted her glass and toasted Caroline with it. "Hear, hear. We should all aim to be more independent."

"Speak for yourself," Joshua said. Jeremy's youngest brother had a lock of red hair that persisted in falling down over his forehead. "I like living at home. Everyone knows what I prefer."

"And aims to please," his father agreed with a smile.

"Because we know what a fuss he'll put up if we don't," his brother Jason grumbled.

Joshua elbowed him in the gut. Jason glared at him.

"Manners," their mother said, and they quickly returned to their food.

Mrs. Willets refocused on Caroline, and she felt the gaze to her toes. She steeled herself for questions about her father. How long before Joy blurted out all she'd heard?

She glanced at the girl, but Joy was busy eating.

"Did you attend school there, dear?" Jeremy's mother asked.

Relief coursed through her along with the excellent stew. "I am a graduate of Miss Wilmont's Academy for Young Ladies. I received high marks for reading and memorization."

All of his sisters sighed in unison.

"Another scholar," his mother said with an arch look to Jeremy. "Perhaps she should talk more with Jacob."

Jacob was only a couple years younger than Jeremy. She located him across the table. Behind his wire-rimmed spectacles, his gray eyes were serious, as if he hoped to learn more about her.

"I'd be happy to exchange thoughts on our favorite books," he offered, leaning forward so that the candlelight glinted on his russet hair. "What are yours?"

Caroline licked the butter off her lips. When it came to reading, the other girls at the academy had preferred adventure or dime novels.

"History books," she said, waiting for the groan that that admittance usually generated. "The founding of our country especially. Thomas Jefferson had a great many things to say that are simply fascinating."

His lean face lit up.

"She's patriotic too," their mother said with another look to Jeremy. "How commendable."

Too late she realized the lady's ploy. This wasn't about making Caroline squirm. This was about showing Jeremy all her finer points. She could have told the dear woman that they'd already covered this in their letters. She'd held nothing back. If she was going to marry a fellow, she'd figured, he ought to know what he was getting.

"I find many things commendable about Caroline," Jeremy said, reaching for the tureen again. "The way she kept her father's house after her mother passed. How she all-but-raised her younger brother in her mother's place. The time she spent soliciting businesses to donate coats and mufflers to protect the poor in the winter."

Oh, right. She had nattered on about all those things. Nevertheless, she felt her cheeks heating as ten more gazes trained her way.

"It didn't seem all that hard at the time," she demurred. "May I have some more of the preserves?"

Jason and Joshua reached for the bowl at the same time, then stopped and narrowed their eyes at each other. Jenny rescued the preserves and passed them to her, a twinkle in her blue eyes.

"Boys," she said.

"Will be boys," Caroline and Jeremy said in unison. She grinned at him, and he grinned back.

Something zinged through her, faster than a bumblebee and sweeter than its honey. She wasn't sure what it was, but she had no intention of questioning it.

He'd known they'd liked her. From the first, her letters had brimmed with enthusiasm and earnestness. She was exactly the sort of girl his mother would appreciate—unafraid of chipping in wherever she was needed. The only mark against her was that he didn't love her.

Yet.

The word hung in his mind as they finished dinner, and he couldn't decide whether it was accompanied by hope or concern. Only Jacob knew of Jeremy's last disastrous attempt at courting. His brother had been there when he'd proposed and been summarily dismissed. He'd thought he had moved past the hurt, but he found the moment still stung.

"Jane and Jacob, you're milking tonight," Ma said, looking at each of them in turn. "Joanna and Joshua have the morning. Jack, who's on duty for the watch?"

"Jeremy and Jason," his brother had said with a look down the table to them.

"Jenny and Joy, I'll need your help in the kitchen tonight and in the morning," his mother continued. "Jane can gather the eggs. Joy can feed the chickens, and

Jacob can slop the pigs and let the other stock out to graze. Jack can tell you the rest of your assignments at breakfast, but I expect Joy, Joshua, and Jason for lessons by mid-morning."

A chorus of "Yes, ma'am" rang out around the table.

"Could I help?" Caroline asked, smile tentative. "I've always enjoyed cooking, and I'd like to learn to take care of the animals."

His mother reached out to pat her hand. "How kind, dear, but completely unnecessary. I want you and Jeremy focused on courting."

So much so that when he rose and started to help clear the table, his mother shooed him out. "See to your bride." She nodded to Caroline. "The stars are out tonight. Should be a good view from the front porch."

In the dark, alone? Oh, his mother was determined to match them up. Next thing he knew, Caroline would be hogtied into marriage like his brother Jesse. She deserved the right to make her own choice.

"Jacob," he called as his brother started down the corridor for the kitchen door. "Come show Caroline the constellations."

A few moments later, Jeremy leaned against one of the porch supports as his brother stood on the edge of the planks and pointed to the stars. Caroline stood dutifully beside Jeremy, gazing up as directed. The candlelight from the parlor window set her black hair to gleaming, and he caught the scent of lavender.

"There must be stars over Cincinnati," he said with a smile.

"Not like here," she corrected him as Jacob stepped down onto the grass. "The city has so much smoke and steam, with lights blazing at all hours, that we often can't see the sky at night." She looked back into the dark. "Here, the stars are everywhere!"

Even in her eyes.

"Technically, the stars are everywhere, everywhere," his literal brother pointed out. "But the ranch has a more unobstructed view than many towns. All those fields." He nodded out across the land.

In the distance, a Ruby Red lowed. Other cows answered. The music of his world.

"Do you need to see to them?" she asked as if she'd heard the sound too.

"Not right now," he answered, turning away from the sparkling view. "We generally let them range, but a few of the other ranchers have spotted rustlers, so we take things in shifts to watch them all night."

"And I should help Jane with the milking," Jacob said. He nodded to Caroline. "I owe you a discussion on literature, Miss Cadhill. Jeremy, remember our lesson."

Jeremy gritted his teeth but managed a nod as his brother continued around the house for the barns.

"Lesson?" Caroline asked.

One of the hardest of his life, but sharing his previous failure at courting wouldn't make this attempt any more successful.

"He's our scholar," Jeremy said instead. "Everything is a lesson to Jacob." He turned for the door in time to see three shapes dart back from the parlor window. So much for privacy!

Caroline must have seen them too, for she shook her head. "Are they all going to play matchmaker?"

"Every last one," Jeremy said. "If you had any ideas of cutting and running, now might be a good time."

Part of him tensed, as if she'd flounce off, but she merely followed him back into the house.

"I like them," she said. "I never had a big family growing up. My father and mother didn't have any siblings, and neither did their parents. For most of my life, it was just me, my father, and Ned."

That sad look was creeping onto her face again,

puckering her brow. Jeremy nudged her with his shoulder. "What's mine is yours. Take my sisters, my brothers, whichever you want. Though I might keep Joy. She's too much fun to let go."

She pursed her lips. "Oh, but I like Joy too. Choices, choices!"

He chuckled and nodded up the stairs, which were lit by an oil lamp at the top. "I need to head for bed. I'm scheduled to take the early morning shift with Jack watching the cows."

"Then I'll head up too."

They climbed the stairs together, and he couldn't help remembering the many times he'd seen his parents do the same. They had slept upstairs before Joshua and Joy had come along, and his father would put his arm around his mother's waist. She'd lean her head against his shoulder. That tenderness and care spoke of a shared love, a commitment.

He slipped an arm about Caroline's waist. She started, but she didn't pull away. It felt right, good.

Like this was where she was meant to be.

She sent him a smile before going into his old bedroom, and he had to force his feet down to the one he'd be sharing with most of his brothers.

They had two cots they used when they had men working at the ranch, like during branding and roundup. Some of his brothers must have brought the cots up, for he found them squeezed into the corners of the room and spread with blankets. His nightshirt was draped conspicuously over one.

He shook his head. He might be the oldest among the brothers still living in the house, but the others were letting him know that that didn't mean he could take one of their beds.

He managed a few hours' sleep on the cot—he'd have to tell Pa they needed better for their workers—then slipped out of the room to help Jack. Jacob grunted in his sleep and tried to turn on the other cot.

"Thought you might have forgotten, what with you courting and all," Jack said when Jeremy rode out to meet him.

"I can watch and court too," Jeremy said. The night was like a velvet cloak about him, soft and dark. The moon had set, but enough starlight trickled down to allow him to spot cattle here and there among the grasses. "Everything looks quiet."

"It always does," Jack said, "until it doesn't. Start the circuit, and I'll meet you on the other side."

With a nod, Jeremy set his horse around the edge of the pastures. Some of his brothers hated the night work, complaining it cut into their sleep. He liked it. With the crickets chirping and the forest whispering, it was a good time to think about his present, about the future.

About Caroline.

She was very much as she'd portrayed herself in her letters, yet he couldn't help wondering about the differences between them. She had only her brother; he was used to a houseful. She'd graduated from a school. They didn't have a school; every claim did its best to teach its own children. They didn't have a church, either, though everyone was hoping the new minister would be able to build one.

"I like your gal," Jack said when they met near the trees on the far side of the pasture. "She seems sensible."

"High praise, brother," Jeremy teased. "Watch out, or I might be jealous."

"You'll have no challenge from me," Jack promised. "When I decide to court a gal, it's going to be one born and raised to ranching."

"Then I wish you luck," Jeremy said. "From what I've seen, the only daughters of ranchers in these parts are younger than Joy, and I'm pretty sure their fathers would disapprove of them starting a courtship."

Jack held up his hand, head cocked. "Do you smell that?"

Jeremy sniffed the air, half afraid of what he might smell, considering the number of cows in the fields around them. But something else drifted from the woods.

"Smoke," he said, tensing. "It's too damp for a wildfire."

"Someone's camping on our land," Jack said, tone darker than the night.

"Might be someone traveling through," Jeremy said, trying to catch sight of the campfire through the trees. "But only a madman would ride into the forest in the dead of night without knowing what he was facing."

Jack settled back in the saddle with a frustrated sigh. "You're right. We'll catch our camper at first light."

That didn't make the next few hours any easier. So much for having time to think. He studied the forest every time he rode past. Jack's head swiveled at any noise. At least the cows didn't seem troubled. Neither did the owl that hooted from the wood every once in a while.

Dawn was a faint glow on the horizon when Jack met up with him, dismounted, and drew his revolver.

"You really think that's necessary?" Jeremy asked as he swung down as well. Their horses moved off to graze.

"You heard the rumors of rustlers," Jack reminded him. "Better safe than sorry."

As the sky lightened, they stepped into the forest. The trees were thick enough here that brush didn't grow easily. The carpet of fir needles muffled their steps, but the small noises fell silent, as if everything tensed to watch them pass. The tang of fir replaced the earthy scent of the cattle, but still, the smoke lingered. Jack seemed to follow it unerringly.

Jeremy's muscles tightened with each step. They should

have gone for reinforcements, but Jack always had to handle everything himself. Normally, he could, but if there really was a gang of rustlers waiting around that next tree…

They came out in a clearing. The charred remains of a fire were scattered among blackened clumps of moss, the smoke twisting up like a silver snake. Jeremy put his back to his brother's, gaze sweeping the area. Nothing moved.

"Gone," Jack said, holstering his gun and moving away from Jeremy. "Must have lit out before dawn." He crouched and studied the ground. "Looks like a bedroll was laid out here."

"Only one," Jeremy said, walking about his side of the campfire. "And those hoof prints are shod."

"Not a native, then," Jack said, rising. "And anyone local would know to build a fire circle to keep the wood dry and the fire from spreading."

"Still might have been someone new passing through," Jeremy insisted as his brother stared into the trees as if he could spot the intruder's retreating back. "Heading for Puget City, maybe? Or west to Olympia?"

"Wouldn't have taken them long to reach Puget City," Jack pointed out. "Why stop here? And if they were heading away, they would have made it farther than the ranch before having to settle for the night." He shook his head. "I don't like it."

"One man a rustling gang does not make," Jeremy countered.

"But one man could be a scout," Jack replied, turning away from the fire. "Best we be on the lookout for trouble."

As if he didn't have enough trouble with his mother and his courtship with Caroline.

CHAPTER FOUR

CAROLINE WOKE TO the sounds of the house stirring. In Cincinnati, she would have been the one to start breakfast, cook it, and clean up from it afterward. She couldn't help feeling as if she were late. She hurried to dress and fix her hair back from her face. Then she clattered down the stairs to the dining room, only to find Jeremy's place at the table empty. The day seemed decidedly less bright.

His mother was no more pleased. Jack and her husband were also conspicuously missing, and Jacob, Jason, and Joshua snatched up a few griddle cakes from the stack and took them along as they escaped with murmured excuses about work that needed to be done.

Mrs. Willets kept glancing at the door to the hallway, then at the case clock against one wall. Caroline tried commenting on the weather, Jane asked her mother's advice on healing chapped hands, Joy and Jenny confirmed their tasks for the day, and Joanna chattered about a new hairstyle she wanted to try. Nothing distracted their mother for long.

Caroline had to admire that. She was easily discouraged when plans didn't go as she'd hoped. It was a wonder her travel from Cincinnati had fared so well. Perhaps that was a sign that this courtship was meant to be.

"I apologize for my son," Jeremy's mother said as his sisters began clearing the table. "I suppose I should apologize for all of them. I made myself perfectly clear that his duty was attending to you." She sent another scowl out the door, as if it would reach each of her menfolk.

"I don't need much attending," Caroline told her. "And I'm not used to being idle. I know you said last night that I should consider myself a guest, but isn't there some way I could help?"

Her face softened. "You're a woman after my own heart, Caroline Cadhill. Very well. Jane and Joanna will be working on the mending this morning. You can help them until Jeremy returns." She pushed off from the table and marched for the kitchen, and Caroline pitied whichever son she found first.

Caroline ventured into the parlor instead, pausing to peruse the bookcase. The Bible, an almanac, adventure novels, and poetry. The girls at the academy had adored Vaughn Everard's romantic works. It was one thing they'd had in common. As soon as they'd realized she could recite each poem from memory, she had never wanted for companions.

She was taking a seat when his sisters came in a few moments later. Jane carried a tall wicker basket piled with clothing, which she set near Caroline before dropping onto another of the chairs. Joanna, his next to youngest sister, set a pincushion, shears, and spools of thread on the side table, then perched on the sofa.

"Thank you for offering to help," Jane told Caroline, selecting a shift from the basket. "Sorry we're only mending today."

"I never was much for embroidery and such," Caroline admitted, "so mending suits me fine."

Jane reached into the basket again, then handed her a

flannel shirt. "This one's Jeremy's. Why don't you start with it?"

She fingered the soft material of the spruce and scarlet plaid. She could imagine him wearing it. The color would bring out the green in his eyes. She turned over the fabric, looking for the spot that required mending.

"You must be very brave," Joanna said as she threaded her needle.

"To come all this way?" Caroline asked, locating a fray in the cuff of one sleeve. Had he torn it working? She could see him out battling the elements trying to save a wounded cow. Funny. When had she decided he was the gallant hero?

"Not just for coming all this way," Joanna said, laughter in her voice. "For coming all this way to marry Jeremy."

Jane tossed another shirt at her. "You like Jeremy best, and you know it."

Caroline turned under the frayed material and began pinning it in place. "I like *my* brother best, but he's the only brother I have. I can't imagine having so many to choose from."

"They each have their gifts," Jane admitted, working on reattaching a strap to the shift. "You'll meet Jesse one day. He's patient and kind, the sort of brother a girl can run and cry to when things go wrong."

Joanna took a slow stitch. "Though he's not the sort to solve problems. You want something done, you go to Jack. He won't stop until the matter is settled."

"But if it's more of a theoretical problem," Jane put in, "you go to Jacob."

"The others call him professor," Joanna told Caroline. "He likes to think he knows it all."

"He knows a great deal," Jane protested. "He applied himself to schooling more than the rest of us combined."

Caroline glanced between them. "Then what do you go to Jeremy for?"

Joanna grinned. "To laugh."

Jane nodded, tugging at the strap as if to make sure it was now secure. "If your heart's broken, if you need to remember there's light in the world, you go to Jeremy. He won't let you languish."

"He'll tease you right out of the doldrums, whether you like it or not," Joanna confirmed.

Jane shook her head. "Listen to us prattling on. What about your brother?"

"Oh, Ned's always good for a laugh too," Caroline said, selecting a needle from the pincushion and setting about threading it. "I'm not sure he takes anything too seriously. I had to watch him all the time when he was little because he'd be the first one to reach too high, run too fast. He skinned his knees and chin more times than I can count. I just wish I knew where he is now."

"Is he missing?" Jane asked, pausing to eye her.

Caroline's fingers froze on the needle. "Did Joy tell you about my father?"

The two sisters exchanged glances.

"Yes," Jane admitted.

"If," Joanna added, "what you said was that he was a noble thief sent to jail because he was too kind."

Caroline smiled as she began sewing. "That's not so far off. Only I don't believe he stole anything." She went on to explain the situation.

"Right after my father was sent away, Ned vanished too," Caroline finished. "No note. No word of explanation. He left one morning, and he never came back."

"How terrifying!" Joanna cried, setting down her work. "What did the sheriff say?"

Caroline refocused on the sleeve. "We have our own police force in Cincinnati. The officer who answered my request said that men leave home all the time, and he had no reason to suspect foul play. He promised to spread the word to watch for Ned, but no one ever reported seeing my brother before I left. I wrote him a note and asked the lodging house owner, Mrs. Potts, to give it to him if he came asking for me. That's the best I could do."

Before Caroline knew what was happening, Joanna surged up and wrapped her arms about her. "Oh, Caroline, I'm so sorry! You must be so worried about him!"

When was the last time anyone had hugged her? Her father had never been demonstrative, and Ned seldom thought to hug her. She closed her eyes and sank into the warmth.

"Thank you," she said as Joanna withdrew to peer into her face hopefully. "I am worried, but I know there's nothing I can do. Ned will have to take care of himself this time."

"Brothers," Jane said with a sigh as Joanna returned to her work. "They can be such a blessing and such a trial!"

They sewed in companionable silence for a few moments, then she tied the thread and bent to bite it off.

"Well, there you are, Jeremy," Joanna said. "Come in and help."

Caroline's head snapped up so fast the string dangled from her lips. He strolled closer and reached out to pull it gently away. His gloved hand brushed her lips, and it was all she could do to force them into a smile.

"Perhaps I should be looking for the shears," he said, "so Caroline doesn't have to work with her teeth."

"I remember seeing them here somewhere," Caroline said. "I was just in a hurry to get it done." She held his shirt high and hoped that it would at least partially cover her flaming cheeks.

"My favorite shirt!" He took it and pressed it against his chest as if it were made of fine velvet. "Thank you."

Caroline ducked her head, pleasure bubbling up.

"I don't recall being thanked for sewing your trousers last week," Jane huffed, "the ones where you ripped open the seat."

Caroline glanced up in time to see red appear on his own cheeks. "My mistake. Thank you, Jane, for not subjecting the family to sights better left unseen." He wiggled his eyebrows at his sister.

Jane gave it up and laughed.

"Have you come to take Caroline away from us, then?" Joanna asked, setting aside her own work. They hadn't made much of a dent in the mending pile, but, she supposed, mending was a constant in a family this size on a busy ranch.

"On Ma's orders," he told them. "Jack and I were a little late coming in this morning, and she met us at the barn. She was rather passionate in her oratory." He leaned closer and lowered his voice. "She even used Jack's middle name."

Joanna giggled.

"It's Hercules," he explained to Caroline as he straightened. "We all find it ridiculous."

"But if Ma uses anyone's middle name," Jane put in, smiling, "we all know we'd better run for cover."

"So, what did Ma want him to do?" Joanna asked.

"Parcel out any chores he had in mind for me to you all," Jeremy replied. "According to Ma, courting takes precedence over every other task for the foreseeable future."

Oh, but she was determined. Caroline wasn't sure whether to be pleased or dismayed. Jeremy had told her a little about the sorts of things he did on the ranch, from milking to rounding up the cattle for branding and driving them to market, to hunting and smoking meat to preserve it.

"But it's spring," she protested. "Don't you have a lot of work to do?"

"Yes, Jeremy," Jane said, shift bunching in her fist, "what about the planting? Jack wants to expand Ma's garden."

"Jack and Jacob will have that in hand," he said, "after consulting the almanac, of course."

"What about hunting?" Joanna asked. "We're all getting tired of ham and jerky. What about a turkey or a goose? Or we could go down to the delta and dig for clams."

"Clams won't be easy to dig until summer," he reminded her. "And Jason's better at hunting than I ever will be."

"Well, you could help with the mending!" Jane threw the shift at him.

He caught it and deposited it back in the mending basket. "Sorry. You're on your own."

Caroline's conscience tugged. "But I promised to help."

Joanna moved the basket closer to her skirts. "No, Ma's right. You're courting. This is Jeremy's turn. We'll have ours one day."

"And don't think we'll forget it," Jane warned. "If I ever enter a courtship, I'll expect you to take over my chores, Jeremy. I'm sure the chickens will love you."

Joanna nodded, then winked at her brother. "For now, you just work on pleasing Caroline."

Pleasing Caroline. Jeremy nearly shook his head. Why did a man have to woo his mail-order bride? She'd already indicated she was willing to entertain the notion of marrying him. She'd come all the way from Cincinnati to meet him!

But Caroline was looking more and more miserable, back hunching and fingers pleating her skirts.

He leaned a hip against her chair. "So, what exactly would please you, Caroline?"

Her brows rose so fast he wondered she didn't get dizzy. "Please me?"

"That's right," Joanna put in. "Tell him how you want him to court you."

Jane nodded her support.

"Well, I," she started. Then she cleared her throat and sat taller. "It's nice when courting couples walk hand in hand together."

He set a hand on her shoulder. "We could do that."

She beamed at him, and he felt very noble.

Joanna set aside her mending. "I always like it when Pa holds Ma's Bible for her during services. And he brings her wildflowers."

"Not quite in season yet," Jeremy allowed, "but I'll keep my eyes open."

"It would be romantic to ride out together for a picnic," Jane said, his practical sister sounding positively dreamy. "Maybe end up at the drop."

Not the drop. "It's too cold for a picnic right now," he reasoned.

"Well, the best part of courting is surely sharing your thoughts and feelings," Joanna said. "Finding another person in complete harmony with you."

Both his sisters sighed, and Caroline gazed up at him, hope in her deep brown eyes.

Sharing every thought and feeling? He didn't do that with his own family! It felt too exposed. He'd opened his heart once, and look where that had led. He no longer believed he'd find anyone in complete harmony with him.

"Let's start with a walk," he said, straightening.

"Give me a moment to fetch my coat," Caroline said.

He waited at the foot of the stairs. He should probably show her the rest of the ranch, but even that felt a little too much like his first attempt at courting.

He and Jacob had attended a church social in Olympia five summers ago. His brother had gone for the lectures by several prominent ministers, including one brought from all the way back East. Jeremy had been more interested in finding a lady. The state capital had a greater number of eligible misses than Hawks Prairie or Puget City.

And there, seated across the aisle of the crowded hall, was a golden-haired beauty with a saucy smile. He began to believe Ma and Pa's story of love at first sight.

"I'm Jeremy Willets," he said as soon as he could make his way to her side. "And if you're not spoken for, I'd like the opportunity to try."

The petite brunette next to her giggled.

"Maisy," his beauty said in a dulcet voice, sky blue gaze on his, "tell Mr. Willets it's customary to be introduced by family or a mutual friend."

Maisy smiled at him as Jacob came up to join them. "I'm Maisy Gallagher, Mr. Willets, and I'm sure we're destined to be friends. So, allow me to introduce you to a great friend of mine, Miss Deborah Morton." She leaned closer and lowered her voice. "Darling Deborah is very popular, but she hasn't settled on a suitor yet."

Which had meant, he'd naively thought, that he stood a chance at winning her heart.

He'd spent the rest of the social living in her pocket, and Jacob had expressed interest in learning more about Maisy, so they had ridden into Olympia twice a week to call on the ladies for over a month. Deborah had been proper, polite, but just warm enough that Jeremy had been encouraged. So, he had invited the pair to see the ranch.

And that was where Deborah's feelings, or lack thereof, had become apparent. He'd been so entranced, he hadn't noticed at first. Looking back, it was easy to recall how cooly she'd spoken with his mother and sisters, eyeing their calico gowns disdainfully. She kept putting her lace-edged handkerchief to her nose as they walked around, as if the normal smells of a ranch overset her.

Maisy had been kinder. She'd turned Deborah's snide

remarks into jokes and expressed her pleasure in her surroundings.

"When you said you were the son of a rancher, Mr. Willets," Deborah had said, adjusting her parasol to better cover her flawless complexion, "I admit I thought your ranch would be more impressive."

He knew a way to impress. At the eastern edge of their property, the land fell away off sharply more than two hundred feet to the valley below, and the Nisqually Delta stretched out like an emerald skirt to the area's glorious lady, Mount Rainier. He and Jacob had escorted their ladies there.

"Oh, how beautiful," Maisy had said, gazing about.

"Yes, it is lovely," Deborah acknowledged.

"No more lovely than you," Jeremy said, going down on one knee in front of her. "You have captured my heart, Deborah, and I'd like nothing more than to spend the rest of my life making you happy. Would you do me the honor of marrying me?"

Maisy gasped. Jacob stared at him as if Jeremy had lost his senses. Perhaps he had, but nothing had seemed more important than to hear her say she felt the same way.

Instead, she gave her parasol a twirl. "You, Mr. Willets, are entirely too precipitous. I think it best if one of your brothers takes me home. You seem to have a number to spare." She turned and started for the house.

He felt as if a horse had kicked in his chest. He could barely struggle to his feet.

"I'm so sorry," Maisy said, wringing her hands though none of this was her fault. "She gets these moods. I'm sure it will pass." She looked to Jacob. "Perhaps you could drive us home?"

Loyal Jacob pushed up his spectacles. "I fear I'm indisposed. But I'm sure one of my *spare* brothers can help."

In the end, Jack had taken them back to Olympia along with the pieces of Jeremy's broken heart.

"We've learned a valuable lesson," Jacob had told him as they'd stood on the porch watching the wagon disappear in the distance.

"Never take a gal to the drop?" Jeremy asked. It was either joke or rail at the world, and he didn't really want his parents or other siblings knowing how far he'd fallen.

"I was thinking more about casting pearls before swine," Jacob had admitted. "The next time we meet likely ladies, we will make sure we know them better before bringing them home. Or proposing."

"Thanks, Professor," Jeremy had said.

It had taken him a few years to build up the will to try again. Deep down, he wanted what his parents had found—companionship, a family. But this time, he'd be the one to call the tune in the courtship.

He'd received several answers to his advertisement for a mail-order bride, but Caroline's had rung truest. Still, he'd asked her about her family, her situation, and what she hoped for in a marriage. He could say what he thought, and yes, what he felt, without anyone complaining that he teased too much or wasn't somehow good enough. The worst that would happen is that she'd stop writing.

And now she was here, and he wasn't entirely sure what to do with her.

CHAPTER FIVE

JEREMY HADN'T EVEN settled on where to take Caroline on their walk before she came down the stairs carrying her coat.

"Allow me," he said, taking the gray wool from her.

She'd tried to put up her hair in a bun at the top of her head, but the thick black tresses were already sliding down toward her nape. He moved them out of the way of her collar. They felt like silk against his fingers. He had to make himself step back and grab his own coat from one of the hooks along the hallway.

"This way," he said, opening the door.

"Will you show me the ranch?" she asked, following him out onto the porch.

She might as well have planted a fist in his gut. He fought off the reaction. He'd invited Deborah to come. Surely, if Caroline was asking, she wanted to see the ranch.

As soon as they stepped off the front porch, he slipped his hand over hers, testing. She didn't pull away. In fact, a smile lifted her rosy lips. Both were good signs.

They walked across the side yard and over to the split rail fence that encircled the pasture. He'd been too little to set it in place the first time. That honor had belonged to Pa and Jesse. But he, Jack, and Jacob had repaired it more times than he could count over the years, and he'd helped expand it to enclose additional pasture and fields.

"From here to the road west," he explained, waving his hand, "to the forest north, the edge of the plateau east, and the blockhouse south, the land belongs to my parents."

She turned in a circle as if to take it all in. "That's a lot of land!"

"Three hundred and twenty acres," he said, finding it impossible to hide his pride in the fact. "Jack's claimed another one hundred and sixty, mostly forest. The bulk of the land is in pasture, though we have a large garden beyond the house and a few fields for hay. Come on, I'll show you."

He walked her past the barns, pointing out the chicken coop, pig pen, sheep pasture, and his mother's garden. It was mostly bare now, with potatoes, turnips, and carrots still growing, along with a few early peas Ma had forced. He even toured her through the shadowy barns.

"We have horses for riding and drawing the wagon or plow," he explained, nodding toward the stalls. "And spots for up to three cows at a time for milking."

"I thought you had cattle for beef," she said, craning her neck as if to see out the door of the barn.

"Mostly," he agreed. "But we have a few cows with calves at any given time throughout the year, and we take turns milking them."

"What a blessing for baking!" She straightened and grinned at him. "Butter! Cheese! Curds!"

His heart lightened. "I'm glad you appreciate it."

"I do," she promised, putting her hand back in his as if she'd been doing it all her life. "We couldn't keep milk in the summer in Cincinnati. Our ice box was too small. So, if I bought some at the market, I had to use it fast. Here, you can use it whenever you like."

They walked back into the sunlight again, and she blinked. Then she drew in a breath. He waited for the complaint.

"And everything smells so good!" she exclaimed.

"Get a little closer to the sheep, and you won't say that," he predicted, still expecting her to turn up her nose.

Instead, she spun in a circle, arms wide, and her skirts belled out under the hem of her coat. "Oh, Jeremy! What a wealth you have!"

He shook his head, relief like cool water on a hot day. "You're a wonder, Caroline Cadhill."

She stopped. "What, me?"

"Yes, ma'am. I don't know anyone except Joy who can take such pleasure in things."

"Well," she said, latching onto his arm with both hands, "maybe I just know a blessing when I see one."

So did he. It humbled him to see the sparkle in her eyes, the tremor of her lips. Did they really have a chance for a life together here?

She tilted her head again as if trying to peer past the barns. "You appear to have only one house, though. Where did you plan for you and your wife to live?"

He nearly missed a step as they started back, and he scolded himself. It wasn't a complaint. She had every right to know what to expect from her future. And he really should have considered the living arrangements before starting correspondence with a mail-order bride. He and his family would need to live somewhere, and, as his mother had just proven by shoving him and Jacob in with Jason and Joshua, the house had precious little room. Why hadn't he thought that through?

Perhaps because he hadn't believed another woman would agree to come to the ranch.

Or that she would stay.

They finished their walk and returned to the kitchen, where Jenny quickly appropriated Caroline. His sister and mother had been baking. Jenny had proven herself a talented cook, so much so that she had started to take over some of their mother's duties.

Ma, on the other hand, seemed torn between quizzing their guest or ordering Jeremy to do something about courting her. In the end, her curiosity must have won, for she handed him a bunch of carrots to peel while the ladies chatted.

Caroline examined the woodstove, shelves filled with preserves, and the pots and pans, and the three ladies discussed recipes and wood smoke and the need for keeping things spotlessly clean. Watching her smile, eyes bright and movements quick and sure, more of the tension leaked out of him. He was so busy watching, in fact, he nicked himself with the peeling knife!

Jacob rescued him before any of the others noticed him fumbling with his handkerchief. His brother had come in from working and stood a moment as if studying Caroline, Ma, and Jenny as he studied one of his beloved books. Then he looked at Jeremy and tipped his head toward the door.

Jeremy joined him in the hallway, tucking his bandaged hand in his pocket. "Everything all right?"

"I was going to ask *you* that question," his brother said, pulling off his wide-brimmed hat. "We haven't had a moment to talk since she arrived. So, you went and did it, wrote away for a mail-order bride."

Jeremy shifted on the plank floor. "I told you I was considering it." Why did he feel guilty? He made himself still.

"And you knew about her father?" Jacob pressed. "Joy had some interesting things to say about him."

"Caroline held nothing back," Jeremy promised him. "To me, or to Joy."

Jacob glanced into the kitchen. "At least she's more interested in the ranch and the family than Miss Morton or Maisy ever was. It gives me hope."

Jeremy too, much as he hesitated to embrace that emotion again.

"Just be careful," his brother warned, gaze coming back to his. "The Bible says we can know people by the fruits they bear. Maybe wait until you see a little more of Miss Cadhill's fruit before proposing this time."

"Now you sound like Ma," Jeremy accused.

Jacob pushed up his spectacles. "I take that as a compliment."

Jeremy smiled, but his brother's warning stayed with him that afternoon as he dutifully trailed after Caroline. Not content to limit their conversation to the cooking, Ma showed her how other things were done around the house. Caroline continued to show her willingness to help by suggesting they add lavender to the wash water (was that why she smelled so good?), offering a recipe for a concoction to add to the liniment chest that would aid sore muscles, and showing Ma how she turned her skirts to save on having to make new ones.

"Good choice, big brother," Jenny murmured to him as they trooped back to the kitchen to finish the dinner preparations. If only he could claim that he'd chosen Caroline and not the other way around.

And so he found himself seated at the dinner table again next to her, placing a slice of venison on her plate from a deer his brother Jason had brought in that day. Jane must have had a talk with him. Jenny had baked oat bread, Caroline had showed her how to mix the butter with apple preserves, and Ma had mashed some of the potatoes.

"Jenny and Joanna, I'd like you to milk this evening," Ma directed. "Take Joy with you. She needs to learn to pull properly."

Joy's lower lip trembled. "I don't want to hurt them!"

"Think how much it would hurt them to carry around a full udder all night," Pa told her. "You're doing them a favor."

"And you're doing us a favor too," Joshua said, reaching for the dish of apple butter again.

"Tomorrow, we'll have a sewing party," Ma continued. "I want that mending done!"

"I'd be happy to help," Caroline put in, and Jeremy resigned himself to another day inside.

"Sorry, Ma," Jack said, slicing into his steak. "We need to paint the barns while the weather is clear. I need everyone's help."

Jeremy winked at Caroline, and she blushed.

"Everyone who isn't courting," he reminded the table at large.

Jack rolled his eyes.

"No," Ma said. "You and Caroline can help as well. It seems to be doing you good to work together."

As if his sisters suspected Jeremy had hoped to avoid the hard work of painting, Jane laughed, and Joanna giggled. Even Jack's smile won free.

His sisters might have high expectations for courtship, but only his mother would think of painting as a way to further romance.

What was next, fighting off rustlers?

What a very pleasant afternoon. Caroline had enjoyed every moment of having Jeremy's mother show her about the house. Many things—like laundry and mending—were the same as what she'd done in Cincinnati, but even similar things were magnified by the sheer number of people! And she had never had to chop wood or slop pigs or gather eggs. It was all fascinating!

"Musical evening tonight," Mrs. Willets declared as Jeremy's siblings cleared the table. "Store Caroline's apple butter for the morning…"

Joshua looked up, pulling a finger that had obviously been in the dish from his mouth. "Apple butter's all gone, Ma."

"I can make more," Caroline offered.

"Perhaps tomorrow," Ma allowed. "Put the dishes to soak, Jane. We'll meet in the parlor."

"Musical evening?" Caroline murmured as Jeremy escorted her down the hallway. "Do you all play instruments?"

"Never had any real instruments," he acknowledged. "I suppose there's spoons or beating on the edge of a table, but that doesn't count. Mostly, we sing hymns and popular songs. Nothing fancy." He cast her a glance as they came into the shadowed parlor. "Likely you had a theater or opera house in Cincinnati."

"Pike's Opera House," she told him as she settled on the sofa and he went to kindle the fire. "I only attended twice. It was very grand, with lots of marble and statues taller than a man, but I found it a little overwhelming to be one of hundreds in the audience."

"Well, we can't hope to match that," he said, gaze on the flickering flame.

He sounded sad, as if sure he had disappointed her.

"I never sang in a group outside of the academy," she tried. "We had music lessons, piano, harp, that sort of thing. We didn't have instruments to practice on at home, so I never became proficient. And I sing in the alto range, so I'm usually the counterpart, not the melody."

He did not seem encouraged as he lit the lamp. When he finally came to sit beside her, his shoulders were tight, and his hands were pressed against the knees of his trousers.

His family began joining them then, so she could not ask what was troubling him. Soon, the parlor was full, with Jenny on Caroline's other side on the sofa, their mother and father on chairs flanking them, and the rest on the remaining chairs. Jack and Jason were missing. They must be watching the cows.

"Do you have a favorite song, Caroline, dear?" Mrs. Willets asked.

If she had, it promptly went into hiding at the back of her mind.

"I'm sure whatever you normally sing will be lovely," she told her.

"'Wait for the Wagon'?" Joy put in hopefully.

"Very well," Ma agreed.

Ned had been fond of the song, so Caroline knew it and could join in easily. With so many voices, hers blended in, and she told herself no one would judge if she missed a note or two along the way. When they finished, Mr. Willets launched into a hymn.

"I need Thee every hour
Most gracious Lord.
No tender voice like Thine
Can peace afford."

Caroline sang along as well, having heard the hymn many times in services. But when they all reached the chorus, as if by silent agreement or long tradition, the family broke into harmony. She could only stop and listen, awed.

"I need Thee, oh, I need Thee;
Every hour I need Thee.

Oh, bless me now, my Savior
I come to Thee."

Mr. Willets took bass, Jacob and Joshua tenor. Jane and Joanna's voices were warm altos, while Jenny, Joy, and Mrs. Willets sang cool soprano. But Jeremy, oh, Jeremy's rich baritone carried the melody. To her, he sounded finer than any singer at Mr. Pike's marvelous Opera House. She could have listened all night.

"Beautiful," she breathed when they finished. "Thank you for sharing that with me."

Now Jeremy stared at her as if she'd been the one to perform so well.

His father chuckled. "You stick with us, Caroline, and you'll find your part as well."

So long as that meant staying at Jeremy's side, she was beginning to believe she would be well content.

The next morning, Caroline hurried through her breakfast of porridge, oat bread, and apple preserves, but the others still beat her out the door. And she couldn't leave the kitchen without asking Jenny whether she'd tried grating cinnamon into the apple preserves.

"Ma usually uses nutmeg," Jeremy's sister said, pulling down one of the golden jars from the shelf and studying it. "But cinnamon would give it a different flavor. I can't wait until the apple harvest!"

"Neither can I!" As soon as the words were out of her mouth, she bit her lip and turned away to go fetch her coat. Until she and Jeremy made up their minds and he proposed, she had no guarantee she would be at the Jumping J until the apples were harvested. Hope felt as fragile as the shell of a robin's egg.

Jeremy was waiting for her just outside the kitchen door. He'd put on a heavy coat and was blowing on his hands. She hugged her coat closer as they started toward the nearest of the two barns. Chickens pecked at the muddy ground under a sky where clouds hovered lower than she'd ever seen.

"You don't get snow this late in the year, do you?" she asked.

"Not usually," he admitted, shoving his hands into his coat pockets. "It's often dry and cold or wet and warm, even in the winter. But every once in a while, we get a storm that piles up the drifts. Ma and Pa still talk of the Blizzard of '64."

She shivered and rubbed both hands up and down her arms. "We can get a foot or more in the winter in Cincinnati, but not this time of year."

Ahead, she spotted his sisters and brothers by the doors of the barn, and her steps slowed. "I don't think I've ever painted anything in my life. Is it hard?"

"Nothing to it," he assured her. "Jack and Jacob will mix up the whitewash and divide it into buckets to pass around to each of us. We just have to use brushes to slosh it over anything that doesn't move."

She smiled at him. "I should be able to handle that."

She nearly changed her mind when they reached the barn. Up close, it towered over her head, and white peeled here and there to reveal strips of weathered gray. Small wonder his brother wanted everyone to help!

All his brothers, all his sisters except Joy, and their father were out in front, and all of them wore heavy canvas aprons over their coats. Jane and Joanna went into the barn, but Jenny held out an apron for Caroline.

"Let me help," Jeremy said, taking the apron and draping it about her. He went behind, then reached around to grab the ties.

Caroline couldn't move as she stood in his embrace, his chest pressed against her back, and his family members watching.

"There," he said, stepping away, and she could breathe again. "I don't suppose anyone brought me an apron."

"You," Jenny said, "know where they're kept. Now, stop dawdling."

"You sound more like Ma every day," Jason said, but he followed her into the barn.

The others turned to go as well. For a moment, Jeremy's smile dipped, and she hurt for him. They hadn't meant to forget him, but she could see why he would see it that way.

She slipped her hand into his. "Perhaps I can paint, and you can direct me. That way you won't get dirty."

He blinked, then shook his head. "You, Miss Caroline Cadhill, are entirely too good to me. But I refuse to stand back like a wastrel while you work. Wait here while I fetch my armor, and then your knight will ride forth to do battle with the barn."

CHAPTER SIX

JEREMY WASN'T SURE which stung more, that his family would forget him in their preparations or that Caroline would imagine he'd be willing to stand and watch while she worked. Did she think him so lazy? Or had the men in her life simply left everything to her?

He had a suspicion it was the latter. From the things she'd written in her letters, her father had spent much of his time working and her brother playing. The cooking, the cleaning, the washing, and everything else in their day-to-day lives they'd left to Caroline. And that wasn't fair.

He might grow frustrated with his family from time to time, but they generally worked together. The ranch wouldn't function otherwise. And there was truth to the saying that many hands made light work.

Just not when those hands belonged to intruders. Before they'd ridden in that morning, he and Jack had made a cursory sweep of the forest as far as the edge of their property, but they'd found no other signs of occupation. Still, they'd alerted Pa and Jacob as soon as they'd returned, and everyone had agreed to remain watchful. They had one hundred head of cattle in the pastures. By many standards, that was a piddling amount, but for them, it was a year's worth of income that supported everything else on the ranch. Losing even a few head would hurt. Whether Ma liked it or not, he had a feeling that keeping the cattle safe would take precedence over courting. And he was surprised that annoyed him more than it should.

Now he located an apron in the bin at the back of the barn and tied it in place before taking Caroline to where his two closest brothers were giving orders. Jack and Jacob had apparently finished mixing the lime-based paint, for they handed out buckets and brushes to their workers, then pointed them to a different p art o f t he barn.

"We're going to start high and finish low," Jacob explained to Jeremy and Caroline as he offered them a bucket and two brushes. "Jason and Joshua will lean out the hayloft doors to reach as much of the top as they can. Jack's going up the ladder to get the rest. I want you two to take the finer work around the bottom doors. Watch out for the hinges. Lime isn't kind to them."

"I understood half of that," Caroline confessed as she followed Jeremy around to the rear of the barn, armed with one of the wide, horse-hair paintbrushes. He led her to where the massive double doors an arm's reach higher than his head stood in the center of the arched wall, with wooden beams crossways to support them and iron hinges clamping them in place.

"Which half?" he teased.

"Door," she said. "Paint. But I'm not entirely sure how they meet."

"Watch me." He set down his bucket, dunked his brush to the top of the bristles, and lifted it dripping to the door. Then he scrubbed it around on the planks, watching as the thirsty wood sucked in the moisture.

"Easy," he said, stepping back. "Just don't get it on anything made of metal, and you'll be fine."

She dipped her brush into the whitewash, dragged it

up, and slapped it on the wood. Paint splattered, hitting Jeremy in the chest, the chin, the cheek. He wiped it off one eyebrow with the back of his hand.

She dropped the brush into the paint with a splash that splattered her apron too and clapped both hands over her mouth. "I'm so sorry!"

"No trouble," he said, lifting a corner of his apron to wipe off the rest. "But I was sure I said to stick to the wood."

She lowered her hands with a giggle. "To be fair, you said don't get it on anything made of metal. I'm fairly sure you're not made of metal, sir."

He might not be made of metal, but he'd thought his heart made of firmer stuff after the debacle with Deborah. He no longer believed he'd look up one day and spot his mythical true love. Too few women. Given the hundreds of lonely bachelors in Washington Territory, any lady here could take her pick, and it wasn't likely to be the third son on a busy cattle ranch, which, apparently, wasn't all that impressive.

But maybe Ma was right about painting being courting, because he could feel his heart opening, softening.

Toward Caroline.

How nice that he wasn't bothered by something so small as splattered paint. Any time she'd answered incorrectly at the academy, Miss Wilmont had looked down her pointed nose and glowered. If Caroline had burned the biscuits or shaken the dust rag too close to the door, her father would sigh, as if he'd hoped for more from her. And Ned would tease her for weeks. He seemed to find it terribly funny that she made mistakes.

Jeremy's teasing felt different, as if it was all right to laugh at mistakes, together.

Nonetheless, she was very careful to keep her paint to the wood of the door after that. She found if she took a moment to wipe the excess off on the rim of the bucket, it was easier to control the flow. And she was pleased to see that Jeremy noticed and mimicked her.

"Fine work," his father said as he came around to check on them. It was the first time she'd seen him walking any distance, and she was surprised to find that he limped.

"We do our best," Jeremy said solemnly, but laughter bubbled in his green eyes.

His father rubbed his hands together. "At this rate, we'll have the whole barn painted by Monday."

Jeremy brightened, until he added, "And then we'll start on the other."

"Always more work to do around here," he said as his father continued on to check the others.

"I like that," Caroline said, dropping her brush in the nearly empty bucket. "You'll never be bored."

"Well, it isn't always the most interesting work," he admitted. Then he winked at her. "But when you have interesting company, it makes it all the easier."

She couldn't agree more.

They all finished in time to clean up at the side of the barn before dinner. Jacob took the brushes to wash them with spirit of turpentine and gave everyone rags soaked in the stuff to clean their hands. The tart piney scent made her wrinkle her nose. She couldn't help wondering who would be given the task of washing all those aprons, but that would likely wait until the painting was over.

Rag in hand, Jeremy stepped closer. "You have two spots, there and there."

She couldn't have seen the spots without a mirror, and she certainly didn't want to go to dinner looking like a speckled hen. She leaned closer, and he dabbed at her cheek. Dark lashes framed his eyes, with tiny creases at the corner, as if he smiled a great deal.

Then their eyes met, and the world faded away. The green seemed to darken as his gaze dropped to her mouth. His lips were only inches from hers.

Caroline closed her eyes, hoping, wishing, and breathed deep.

Inhaling a lungful of turpentine fumes.

She choked and coughed, her eyes popping open and her whole body shaking.

He straightened and patted her back. "Are you all right?"

"Fine," she wheezed. "I'll see you in the house."

She fled before he could respond.

Like his sisters, she'd dreamed of being courted for years. Walking hand in hand to services with someone who admired her, just as she was. Dancing in her beloved's arms. Sitting in the parlor by a warm fire and talking long into the night. Kissing goodnight on the porch and going to sleep with the joy of knowing he'd be back tomorrow.

She hadn't even managed a kiss in the barn! And she was supposed to be a mail-order bride!

Jeremy was trying to do his part in courting. She should do the same. She could support him as she wished to be supported, think of things that might please him too.

She made sure to check her hair and face, then hurried into the kitchen, where Jenny was taking golden-topped biscuits from the oven.

"What's Jeremy's favorite food?" Caroline asked.

Jenny raised her brows, then giggled. "Oh, I see. You want to cook him something."

Caroline nodded.

Jenny leaned closer. "He's quite partial to strawberry rhubarb pie, but we won't have fresh for a while. Can you make do with canned?"

"I'll have to compensate for the extra liquid," Caroline mused, finger tapping her chin. "But I think I can contrive."

"We'll do it tomorrow, then," Jenny promised, straightening. "We can serve it for Sunday dinner."

They grinned at each other.

Dinner was much easier to eat after that. Jenny and his mother had made fried chicken, biscuits, and mashed turnips, and platters flew up one side of the table and down the other as soon as Mr. Willets had said the blessing. Once again, Jeremy served her, as if she were a princess and he a courtier bent on flattery.

But it was clear that wasn't sufficient for his mother.

"You all made such good progress today. I see no reason why Jeremy and Caroline cannot be excused when you resume painting on Monday," she said as they tucked into the meal. She looked to Jeremy. "You should show Caroline more of the area. The lake, perhaps."

"It's more of a pond than a lake," Jeremy confided with a smile that nearly made her forget about the food before her.

"And it's only fun to swim in when the weather's warmer," Joshua shot across the table. "And the cows haven't beaten you to it."

Jeremy winked at her, and that tingly feeling started all over again.

"The blockhouse would be a better choice," Jacob suggested. "It has historical importance."

"Anything older than you has historical importance in your mind," Jason pointed out. "I'd take her to the drop."

Joanna and Jenny giggled. Jeremy flushed and looked away.

Interesting.

"I'd like to see this drop," Caroline said. "It sounds mysterious. And the blockhouse too." She smiled at Jacob, but he was watching Jeremy.

"That's settled then," his mother said, passing Joshua the turnips, which he had somehow neglected to add to his plate. "We'll be busy with services tomorrow, but

Monday you can saddle two of the horses and have a nice ride, weather permitting."

"Barometer indicates a clearing trend," Jacob offered. "It should be a sunny day."

Caroline reached for her glass. "I've never ridden a horse."

All conversation ceased, and silver clanked on porcelain as someone dropped a fork.

"Never?" Joy asked, wide-eyed.

Jane and Jenny looked positively shocked, as if she said she would walk to church in her underthings. Jason was scowling as if this proved she was irreparably damaged. Their father's lower lip was out, as if he pitied her. She wanted to crawl under the table.

"No, sorry," she mumbled. "I had no need back home. Everywhere I went was a short enough distance to walk. And when it wasn't, Father borrowed a carriage."

"I'll teach her," Jack said as if that was that. "It's not hard, Caroline. I'm sure you'll catch on quickly."

"I should teach her," Jacob corrected him, shoving his spectacles up his nose. "You call me professor, after all. That's what professors do: teach."

"And what do you two know about riding sidesaddle?" Jane challenged. "Joanna and I may ride astride when we're helping with the cattle, but Caroline will want to ride like a lady."

"Which is why *I* should teach her," Jenny put in. "She's closer to my size and could use my saddle."

Arguments sprang up on all sides. Caroline blinked in surprise.

Jeremy put a hand on hers and gave it a squeeze. "I'll teach Caroline," he announced over the top of his squabbling siblings. "It would be my pleasure."

With him looking at her so warmly, it would be her pleasure too.

Everyone settled down after that, so Caroline was able

to enjoy the rest of the meal. Still, the idea of doing something more for Jeremy teased her mind. The first night she'd been here, he'd taken her out to look at the sky. She could invite him to do that again. A kiss under the stars? What could be more romantic?

But his mother had other ideas for the evening. She handed out her usual tasks for the morning, then asked everyone's help in getting ready for services in the morning.

"Carry your chairs into the parlor," she directed. "Jason, Joshua, fetch those two benches you use in the barn. Joy, find quilts to pad and cover them. We'll put them under the window, at the back."

"You don't have a church?" Caroline asked Jeremy as she carried her chair toward the parlor.

He glanced back over his shoulder from where he was carrying his own chair. "Not yet."

His mother, who was supervising from the doorway, must have caught the exchange, for she chimed in. "Mr. Dalrymple, our minister, is hoping to raise funds to build one. As it stands, the ranches and farms take turns hosting services, and it's our turn tomorrow. And we want to make sure everyone is comfortable."

It was a scurry and a hurry, but soon, the parlor boasted several rows of chairs and benches of one kind or another, and the sofa held pride of place at the front, next to a table and the spot where the minister would stand.

She sidled closer to Jeremy as he stepped away from the sofa. "Looks like a nice night out there." She tipped her head toward the porch.

His smile grew. "Mighty fine night. Perhaps we should…"

"I have to apologize, Caroline," Jacob said, joining them. He must have knocked his spectacles loose in all the hurry, for he settled them more firmly on his nose now. "I owe you a discussion of literature."

Disappointment nipped. But, much as she wanted to spend time alone with Jeremy, she certainly didn't want to antagonize any member of his family. And how long could it take to talk about books? "Why, certainly, Jacob."

"Now you've done it," Jeremy warned. "He can go on for hours."

Oh, dear.

Jacob drew himself up. "I'll have you know that a well-read mind is a treasure."

"It certainly is," Caroline agreed. "I saw a number of fine books on your shelves. Which are your favorites?" That should be a safe gambit. How many favorites could he have?

Quite a few, as it turned out, though most had a scientific bent, like *Frankenstein* and the works of Jules Verne.

"And yours, Jeremy?" she asked when she could get a word in edgewise.

"Anything that's short," he joked.

"My brother isn't the most patient when it comes to learning," Jacob explained. Then, as if realizing he wasn't helping with courtship by maligning Jeremy, he hurried on. "That is, not all of us are gifted in every area. I have found Jeremy to be neat in his habits and encouraging in his conversation."

"Such praise, brother," Jeremy quipped.

"High praise indeed," Caroline countered. "What bride doesn't want a husband who is neat and encouraging?"

Jeremy raised a brow. "I had no idea those were high on your list of qualities in a husband."

"I never made a list like some girls do," she allowed. "But I'd have to say kindness and encouragement would be requirements."

He nodded slowly, as if she'd revealed something important, then exchanged glances with his brother, who also nodded. Her whole face felt on fire. She was just glad his mother declared it time for bed before either Jeremy or Jacob could question her further.

She puffed out a sigh as she shut the bedroom door. Should she have a longer list of requirements? A hard worker, perhaps, someone who would provide for his family? What had she been looking for when she'd read those mail-order bride ads? A husband, certainly. But some of the ads had been easy to avoid.

Wanted: wife willing to work hard and raise six children.

She hadn't been clear whether the fellow wanted six children or already had six children, but either way, he had made it sound as if she'd be doing the raising alone. She already did everything around the house alone. Shouldn't she look for a better situation, not more of the same?

Wanted: woman willing to move to Wyoming Territory and help with claim. Marriage optional.

No, marriage was a requirement!

Wanted: good-natured bride willing to relocate to Washington Territory and make a home with lonely cattle rancher. Offering companionship and a helpmate in times of trouble.

Jeremy's ad had caught her eye from the first. She was good-natured, willing to relocate, and happy to make a home, so she appreciated and met all his criteria. Loneliness, she understood. Companionship and a helpmate sounded wonderful!

She hadn't thought much beyond that until his letters had started arriving, and the man they revealed met every criterion she didn't know she had.

But his mother was right. Letters might not tell the truth. They were words, after all. She must watch his actions.

And show by her own what she expected and valued.

CHAPTER SEVEN

THE NEXT MORNING, she rose early, determined not to be the last downstairs. She dressed in her best gown, a pale pink silk that boasted an overskirt, cuffs, and a long bodice edged in a wide, fluted ruffle. She hadn't asked about an iron to press the fabric, so it was fairly rumpled from her valise. As it was, she'd only had room to bring two dresses with her besides the one she had been wearing.

Someone rapped on the door, and she opened it to find Joanna waiting. She too must be wearing her best, for she was gowned in a spring green lustring with a nipped waist and embroidered vines all along the hem. Hair hanging in wild disarray about her face, Jeremy's sister held up a silver-backed brush.

"Trade?" she suggested. "You help me with my hair, I'll help you with yours."

"Done," Caroline agreed, holding the door open to let her in.

Joanna glanced around, then perched at the end of one of the beds. "Of course—no dressing table for my brothers. But they don't feel the need to look their best."

Caroline pulled her brush carefully through the curly reddish-brown tresses. "Does everyone expect us to look our best?"

"Ma will," she predicted. "She always says we should wear our best clothes to church, though I'm pretty sure God doesn't care how we look so long as we draw near." She smiled. "My hair has a mind of its own, but pull it up and back as best you can and let the curls fall as they may. I brought pins." She began pulling them from the pocket of her gown.

Caroline set to work, marveling at what she'd said. Church back home had been as much about being seen as listening to the sermon. Her father had always seemed embarrassed when they sat in their usual pew below the middle of the church, as if that somehow reflected on their place in life. How wonderful that she didn't have to be the cleverest, loveliest, or wealthiest to be loved by God!

She finished with Joanna's hair and took her turn on the bed.

"How would you like it?" Joanna asked, running the brush briskly through Caroline's hair.

She made a face. "I don't know."

"Not to worry," Joanna assured her. "I've been studying fashion plates. My new sister-in-law Alice brought some with her last time she visited. She has a friend named Beth who dotes on *Godey's*."

She was almost glad the only mirror in the room was small and located some distance from them, so that she didn't have a chance to see what Joanna was doing. Jeremy's sister was putting in the last pin when Jane poked her head into the room.

"Ma says downstairs by a quarter past."

"Almost done!" Joanna promised. She stepped back and nodded toward the mirror. "See what you think."

Caroline scrambled for the mirror. Joanna had pulled her hair up and back too, so that it cascaded down behind her in dark waves. What was left framed her face and made her eyes look huge. She touched her temple. "I love it! Thank you!"

Turning, she hugged the girl close.

Joanna hugged her back, then stepped away, silvery gray eyes twinkling. "Let's see how Jeremy likes it."

Jeremy couldn't stop staring as Caroline sat beside him for worship services. From the day she'd walked into the parlor, he'd thought her pretty. But with her hair fixed to highlight those big brown eyes of hers and in a fancier dress that fit her properly in all the right places?

Well, she was stunning!

He was glad he'd offered to sit on the barn benches under the window during the service with Joshua and Jason. Covered with some of his mother's quilts, the boards were comfortable enough, but most of their neighbors had opted for the chairs or sofa, which meant they were sitting in front of him and Caroline. The bachelors had to turn completely around, and risk their neighbor's wrath in the process, to eye her.

He tucked her arm in his nonetheless.

Mr. Dalrymple stood at the front, Bible open on the side table, as he led them in worship. He was square-jawed and solid-framed, and he had a habit of nodding to emphasize a point. His brown hair didn't so much as bob in the process, slicked back as it was with pomade. Jeremy had never tried the stuff. Jack had experimented with it at one point and warned them all away.

"Most of us have had a brush with death," the minister said now. "Perhaps a loved one snatched away too soon, a friend lost."

He hadn't, and that was a blessing. Yet Caroline had lost her mother. He glanced her way, but she was listening, gaze fastened on the preacher, as if she was memorizing each word for consideration later.

"We know the pain and sorrow of loss," Mr. Dalrymple continued. "Imagine if there was a physician in the area, a man known for healing the sick, sometimes miraculously. And imagine you'd sent for him, but he never came. Would you blame him for the death of your beloved? Would you shout at him the next time you saw him, berate him for his absence?"

He nodded around.

Caroline nodded as well. Jeremy tried to imagine the scene taking place in his family. It wasn't hard, although shouting and berating were more Jack's style than his. In fact, since he'd turned sixteen, he'd looked on it as his role to keep Jack from getting too serious, especially about little things. His contribution to keeping the peace.

Huh. Maybe he was more like Pa and Jesse than he'd thought.

"Now Mary and Martha, the sisters of Jesus's friend Lazarus, had hoped for a miracle too," Mr. Dalrymple said. "Our Lord could have saved their brother. But when Lazarus died, they lost that hope. Death was final. The last word." He leaned forward as if to tell them a secret. "Isn't it funny how we tell ourselves stories all our lives, and they turn out not to be true?"

Jeremy frowned as the minister went on to relate how Jesus had raised Lazarus from the dead. Much as Jeremy liked to joke and tease, he couldn't find the humor in someone spending their entire lives believing a lie.

Something nudged him, and he glanced at Caroline, but she hadn't moved from her rapt contemplation of the minister. Jason had leaned back and closed his eyes, for all Ma would have swatted him if she'd been in arm's reach. Joshua frowned at Jeremy as if wondering why his brother was regarding him.

Jeremy shook his head and faced front again. He refused

to think that nudge had come from his conscience. He hadn't believed any lies after Deborah had shown her true colors. He knew who he was now, what he wanted. That was what mattered.

Just help me through this courtship, Lord. That's all I ask.

Caroline drew in a breath as the minister said the benediction. Such a nice service. The smaller number of people and the parlor setting made it feel more intimate. Mr. Dalrymple had a way of speaking, without the fancy phrasing their minister in Cincinnati had insisted upon, that brought the stories in the Bible more vividly to life.

Sitting next to Jeremy made the whole service even better. She'd caught him nodding along with her, as if he agreed to the same points she did. And he'd kept an eye on his younger brothers too.

Of course, she was beginning to realize, everything was richer when Jeremy was beside her.

"A few announcements," Mr. Dalrymple said as everyone settled back in their seats. "Mrs. Larsen is expecting her first child, and Mrs. Willets has kindly offered to help prepare some clothing and sundry. Apply to her if you're handy with a needle."

He hadn't said to apply to her *if you are female*. She could count the number of women outside the family and her in the room on one hand. And bachelors probably knew how to at least sew on a button.

Ned hadn't. He'd left all such things to her. Her throat tightened. Was he worshipping somewhere today? Was he safe? Was he even alive?

She shook herself before tears could fall and focused on the minister again.

"Just as importantly," he said, "Mr. Henshaw has decided to move to greener pastures and has generously offered to sell his fine house and acreage on the bluff above Puget City to us at a pittance of the price so we can build a church, provided we come up with the money by June."

Murmurs echoed, along with a smattering of applause.

Mr. Dalrymple held up his hands. "Unfortunately, there's still the matter of the pittance. We'll be taking up a collection today and every week. I'd appreciate it if you spoke to your employers and any others you think might be willing to donate."

He nodded to a boy in the first row, who rose and started passing around a hat.

"Sure would be nice to have a church," Joshua said from beyond Jeremy. Both his youngest brothers were in brown suits, their hair neatly combed, even Joshua's cowlick.

Jason leaned back as far as the window behind them would allow. "Nothing wrong with worshipping in a parlor."

"You only say that because you're too poor to contribute," Joshua jibed.

Jason stiffened. "So are you."

"Says who?" The youth pulled a coin from his trouser pocket. "I still have two bits from my birthday."

The boy with the hat had reached the back and held it out hopefully. Joshua dropped in his gift. The boy looked to Caroline.

"Sorry," she murmured. "Perhaps next time."

"Consider this a donation from us both," Jeremy said, adding a gold piece to the pile.

The boy smiled, then looked to Jason, who waved him away.

"Much obliged," he said before returning the hat to the minister.

The other members of the congregation were rising again and exchanging greetings. Jeremy rose as well, offering Caroline his arm.

"You've been spotted," he warned as several men headed their way.

Once more he sounded more serious than she would have expected.

"Should I defend myself or flee?" Caroline teased, hand on his arm.

He put his hand over hers. "I'll defend. You flee." He nodded to the open parlor door beyond Jason and released her.

But it was too late. A man who looked nearly her father's age stuck out his hand, preventing her from moving. He didn't wait for Jeremy to introduce him either.

"I'm Jim Ballus," he said, smoothing back what was left of his hair with his free hand.

A younger man with bright blond hair blocked her on the other side. "And I'm Brett Hartley. I run the Lakeside Ranch down the road a piece."

"Your father runs it," Jason seemed to feel compelled to put in. "You help."

Hartley colored. "Pa leaves most of the work to me these days. Unlike your pa, he doesn't have a pack of pups running around with nothing better to do than carp."

Jason surged to his feet.

Jeremy stepped neatly in front of him as if to prevent a confrontation. "This is Miss Cadhill. She was just leaving." He tipped his head toward Jason and Joshua, but his brothers showed no inclination to take the hint and help her out.

"What brings you to this fair country, Miss Cadhill?" Mr. Ballus asked.

Caroline looked to Jeremy. Would he want her to claim an engagement when they hadn't settled the matter between them? Rumors like that could force him to the altar, if for no other reason than to save his reputation and hers. But he was watching the men with narrowed eyes.

"I corresponded with Mr. Willets here," she told them.

"And his description of Washington Territory made me want to see it for myself."

"Never knew you were such a gifted writer, Willets," Mr. Ballus said.

"Any man can be a poet about a subject he loves," Jeremy replied. His look came back to her, once more so admiring that she couldn't meet it for more than a moment.

That's when she noticed three more men crowding behind the others, faces eager. Mr. Hartley stepped closer, as if determined to prove that he'd staked his claim first.

Jeremy put a hand on her elbow. "It was good to see you, gents. Excuse us."

He ushered her out of the room to a chorus of protests.

"Won't they think you unneighborly?" she asked as he whipped open the front door and nearly pushed her through.

"Very likely," he said. "But I'm taking no chances where you're concerned."

Caroline glanced back. Three faces were pressed to the window, watching them: Mr. Ballus, Mr. Hartley, and a man she didn't recognize.

"Why are they so intent?" she asked, picking her way down the steps instead. Several wagons stood waiting, their horses having been let into various pastures to graze.

"You're the prettiest girl to show up in these parts in months, maybe years," Jeremy answered. "You can't blame them for trying."

She jerked to a stop, letting her skirts fall. "You mean they wanted to *court* me?"

"Court you, marry you, take you home," he answered. "Good thing you already agreed to my courtship, or you'd be under siege."

He seemed determined to spirit her away nonetheless. Caroline shook her head as they started around the side of the house. "But Jane, Jenny, and Joanna are old enough to marry. They're all prettier than me."

He grinned at her. "I'm their brother, so it's not for me to comment on their looks. But if you ask me, you'd have to travel a far piece to find someone prettier than you."

That couldn't be right. Back home, she could throw a rock and hit a girl prettier than her. Prettier, better connected, wealthier.

"How many eligible brides live near Hawks Prairie?" she asked, picking up her skirts once more to detour around an industrious hen.

"If you mean unmarried, unbetrothed females over the age of eighteen and not currently employed in questionable activities, three," he said. "And you've met them."

"Your sisters?"

"That's it. Puget City has a few more, but they tend to marry men who work there. Olympia is better favored, but it's too far to travel very often. Makes it difficult for courting. You can see why I wrote away for a mail-order bride."

"I certainly can!" She could also see something else, and it shook her. The girls back home would never have mentioned the matter, but she couldn't live a lie.

"But that means you also have a choice," she made herself say, each word like a blow to her heart. "If all those men are interested in courting me, you don't have to. Not unless you really want to."

She was right. If Jeremy had had any doubts, if he'd wanted to stop his mother's interference, all he had to do was introduce her to one of the other bachelors. Deborah had had dozens of suitors. Some days, when he'd called on her, four other men were already in attendance.

Then he'd felt awed she'd allow him to be one of them and confident she'd choose him in the end. Now he realized she'd reveled in the power and held off making a decision as long as possible, looking for the perfect groom.

And he'd never stood a chance.

Caroline, on the other hand, seemed genuinely shocked and a little dismayed to find herself suddenly so popular. She was giving him an opportunity to back out, but she didn't seem pleased by the thought. Her pretty face had paled, and she worried her lower lip.

Some might consider it only fair to give the other bachelors a chance at winning her heart. But not Hartley—he was barely out of the schoolroom. And Ballus had already worked two wives to their deaths. In fact, Jeremy couldn't think of one bachelor of his acquaintance who was good enough to marry Caroline.

Even, he was beginning to think, him.

So, he winked at her as they came around the back of the house. "Oh, you can't get rid of me that easily. Ma would never forgive me if I didn't give courting my all."

For some reason, that didn't seem to satisfy her, for she kept watching him as if expecting him to wipe his hand across his forehead in relief that he no longer had to bear the burden of her. As if she were any kind of burden to begin with.

"Caroline!" Joy's voice sailed across the yard, and they both turned to find her skipping toward them. That girl. She didn't sit when she could hop, didn't walk when she could skip. Of all of them, she was the most aptly named.

"Ma needs you," she announced as she came to a stop in front of them. "She's talking with Mrs. Abercromby about ways to raise money for the church, and she said you'd have ideas, on account of you helped get coats for the poor back home."

"I'd be happy to help," Caroline said, and she hurried

off with his sister as if a wolf had come prowling out of the forest.

Or she feared Jeremy was about to propose.

CHAPTER EIGHT

CAROLINE AND JOY went through the kitchen door just as Jack came out. The rest of the congregation was likely gathering horses and harnessing teams, but Jeremy's brother had already changed into his work clothes, and everything from the determined look on his face to his swift stride spoke of purpose. Jeremy swallowed a sigh and widened his stance.

"It's Sunday, Jack," he said. "A day of rest and reflection, according to Ma and the Bible."

"The good Lord didn't run a cattle ranch," Jack retorted, but he glanced back at the house as if fearing to see Ma coming after him with the rolling pin.

Jeremy crossed his arms over his chest. "No, He only created the world and everything in it. I figure since He could take a day off, so can we."

Jack drew abreast. His hair might be the same fiery red as Jane's, but it had been cut short and his chin was clean shaven, as if he didn't brook any nonsense even from his hair. "I was going into the woods again to make sure we don't have more company we didn't expect."

"No one's smelled smoke or spotted a stranger," Jeremy reminded him.

"Our stranger may have gotten better about hiding his tracks," Jack replied.

Jeremy had had in mind to spend his afternoon with Caroline as soon as he could pry her free from his mother. Maybe they would take a walk, and he could hold her hand. Maybe he'd show her the pond.

Maybe she'd let him kiss her.

Where had that thought come from?

Time to consider later. For now, Ma had appropriated her, and he couldn't let Jack head off to meet an unknown number of possibly dangerous men all by himself.

"Give me a moment to change," Jeremy said. "I'll come with you."

Jack's smile hitched up.

A short time later, the two of them strode out across the fields toward the forest. Jacob had been right—the sun was out. The clouds were running for the mountains, leaving the fields sparkling clean and bright green. It would have been a perfect day for walking or riding with Caroline. He cast a glance back at the house.

"You like her," Jack said.

Jeremy chuckled. "Perceptive, brother. Was it the way I stare at her like a starving man or how I keep within three feet at all times?"

"Neither," Jack said, gaze on the trees as they approached. A few of the Ruby Reds raised their heads to watch them. "You've always been quick to deflect questions with a quip, except when it comes to her. You actually talk to Caroline."

"I talk to you," Jeremy insisted. "You just don't listen to what I have to say."

"I listen," Jack said. "I don't always agree, but I listen." He paused at the edge of the woods and peered into the shadows.

Jeremy drew in a breath through his nose. "No more smoke than usual, and likely coming from the house."

"Agreed," Jack said. For a moment, Jeremy thought that

might be enough to satisfy his brother. But Jack plunged into the shadows, and Jeremy followed.

They wound their way through the trees, brushing against sword ferns as high as their waists. The mossy ground quieted the sound of their steps, so that he could hear the twitter of birds in the distance. The air smelled of decaying wood and new growth.

Jack went silently, as much to keep from alerting any enemy as the fact that he preferred silence. Jeremy's mind drifted. Courtship, mail-order brides, and stories that might not be true, like his parents' belief in love at first sight. Like his belief that Deborah had cared.

Suddenly, Jack surged to the right. Jeremy changed course to match. They crashed through the brush into a clearing where bracken had been uprooted and trampled.

Jack turned in a circle, gaze spearing into the forest.

Jeremy crouched by a pile of charred branches. "Cold. Whoever built this has been gone hours, maybe a full day."

Now Jack's gaze swept the ground. "Looks like three people tried to bed down, there, there, and there. Wasteful. They could have used the bracken to cushion the ground. Instead, they just shoved it aside. So, did our first stranger send for friends?"

"Or are these two groups?" Jeremy countered, rising.

Jack shook his head. "Either way, I don't like it. There's a perfectly good road to Puget City and Olympia. No one has any reason to ride through our land, much less camp without permission."

"It's not like there's a sign," Jeremy pointed out, waiting to see what his brother planned to do next. "The forest track isn't even fenced. They might not have known they were on our land. Not everything is a danger, Jack."

"And not everything is safe either," Jack replied, turning away. "We'll add a watch on the cows during the day and double the watch at night."

Jeremy frowned, following. "For how long?"

"As long as it takes to make sure these rustlers are gone." Jack cast him a glance. "We'll need your help too."

"You have it," Jeremy assured him. "Even though I'm still not convinced you need it. Maybe we should talk with Pa first."

Jack kept his gaze on the brush as they cut through the forest. "I'm trying to spare Pa as much as possible. He's not well, Jeremy."

Jeremy grabbed his brother's shoulder to stop him. "What do you mean? Pa looks fine."

Jack met his gaze. "He limps. He gets tired a lot faster than he used to. Doc Rawlins said his heart isn't as strong as it should be."

His jaw felt as if it were made of rock. "Why am I hearing about this now?"

"Pa didn't want to worry anyone. Ma is concerned enough as it is. You've seen how she's taken to giving everyone orders. I figured if I stepped up, if I took on more of the work, he could rest."

So, that's why his brother had been driving himself, and the rest of them, so hard.

Jeremy released him. "So, we don't tell Pa. If you need help, come to me."

"I thought you were courting," Jack said. "Riling up Ma isn't going to give Pa any rest."

"You leave Ma to me," Jeremy said as they set out again. "I can manage courting and caring for my family at the same time."

"It's not that easy," Jack said, skirting a massive boulder. "I haven't even found a way to go courting."

"For which the ladies in Puget City and Olympia are grateful," Jeremy told him with a grin.

"Joke all you like," Jack retorted. "Jane, Jenny, and Joanna will be marrying in the next few years. Ma's going to need help too. A wife who understands ranching would be a benefit."

"Maybe you haven't been paying attention," Jeremy said, ducking under a low-hanging branch. "Ma expects you to marry for love, not for her benefit."

"Who says I can't do both?" Jack challenged. "I'm not planning on writing away for a mail-order bride. I'd rather meet a gal first and get to know her by her actions rather than her words."

Jacob had said much the same. But Caroline's letters had carried more than words—they'd carried hopes, fears, dreams. And now that she was here, her actions matched what he'd gleaned. She was a fine woman, someone who would make an excellent wife.

And others were already noticing.

Caroline spent part of the afternoon with Jeremy's mother and sisters, planning ways they could raise money for the new church. It was the least she could do, having no funds to contribute. Then she and Jenny worked on the pie for dinner, bringing it hot from the oven just before they all sat down. The crust was golden brown, the scents exactly what she'd hoped when she'd grated the spices into the fruit mixture.

Jenny licked her lips. "He'll love it!"

She could only hope.

The one thing that had made the afternoon less enjoyable was that she missed spending time with Jeremy.

Funny—she'd had only his words for the last three months. When had his presence become so important to her?

She was used to the dinner routine by now. His father said the blessing, and bowls and platters began flying. Jeremy encouraged her to fill her plate and joined in the conversation, but he didn't joke nearly as much, and his gaze kept drifting to his father.

She couldn't imagine they'd had an altercation. His father had been even-tempered in his dealings with her. Was he more stern than he'd seemed?

She studied the family patriarch between bites of biscuit. Were there more lines around his eyes? A gray tinge to his skin? He seemed to be picking at his food, but maybe chicken stew wasn't to his liking.

Would he like the strawberry rhubarb pie any better?

Jenny brought it out as the rest of the meal ended. Her smile lit the room as she set it down in front of Ma. "Courtesy of Caroline," she said with a wink to her.

"How lovely!" Ma exclaimed. "Pass your plates for a piece."

She'd been amazed by how quickly the family passed their serving bowls during a meal. Now she barely caught sight of the plates as they zoomed down the table. Her plate came back just as quickly. She cut into the pie. Firm crust top and bottom. Good. Not too much liquid. Better. She put a forkful in her mouth. Spices about right, but maybe she should have added a little more sugar. The strawberries here were all wild and smaller than she was used to.

Jeremy groaned.

Her hopes plummeted, and she chanced a glance in his direction. His head had lolled back on his neck, and he was eyeing heaven as if suspecting it had arrived on their doorstep.

"Good?" she asked, afraid to hear the answer.

He swallowed, meeting her gaze. "Delicious! Thank you so much!"

She drew in a breath, smiling back. "You're welcome. Jenny told me it was your favorite."

"A favorite and not one easy to make around here," his mother confirmed. "Nicely done, Caroline, dear."

And if that wasn't fine enough, Mrs. Willets even allowed Caroline to help clear the table, as if she were no longer just a guest.

"I knew Jeremy would like it," Jenny said as Caroline set a stack of plates near the big porcelain sink that stood under the window.

"We all enjoyed it," Jack put in, passing on the way to the back door. "Nice to have another good cook in the house."

Caroline fanned herself with her hand as he exited. "I don't think I've heard so much praise my whole life, and all over a pie!"

"Not just a pie," Jane said, coming in with a pile of serving bowls. "You have a commendable attitude, Caroline. We all feel it."

She glanced to the door to the hallway, where Jeremy stood waiting.

"Go on," Jenny said with a grin. "Jane and I can handle the rest."

"You have the most marvelous family," Caroline told him as they started for the parlor.

"You'll get no argument from me there," he said. "And you didn't have to cook for me, but I'm glad you did. You know what you're doing in the kitchen."

Much more of this and her chest would be so puffed she'd no longer fit in her clothes.

"I had to learn fast," she explained. "My mother showed me a few things before she died, but Father just expected me to carry on with the cooking afterward. I experimented a lot over the years."

"You can experiment on me any time," he promised her.

The rest of his family joined them a short time later. Because it was Sunday, Jack had agreed to start the evening cattle watch a little later so everyone could be together for a bit. Joshua and Jason brought in chairs from the dining room. Caroline wasn't sure what was planned, but Jeremy's family seemed to be watching Mrs. Willets on her seat on the sofa.

"Storytelling tonight," she declared.

Someone grumbled.

Their mother ignored the sound. "Your task is to think of a tale to encourage and inspire."

Joy, who was sitting next to her, wiggled closer. "May I go first, Ma? Please?"

Mrs. Willets smiled at her. "Yes, you may, Joy."

Joy beamed, then glanced around at her family. Clasping both hands in front of her gingham dress as if she couldn't contain her delight, she raised her head.

"Once upon a time," she said, "there was a family that lived on a big ranch in Washington Territory."

Jeremy leaned closer to Caroline and lowered his voice. "Stop me if you've heard this one before."

She bit her lips to keep from giggling.

"They had lots of cows," Joy continued, "and some horses and the cutest sheep."

"Only you think the sheep are cute," Jason informed her.

Joy scowled at him. "This is my story."

"Let her speak, Jason," Mr. Willets put in.

Jason subsided with a nod.

"They also had pigs and chickens," Joy said, a dreamy smile replacing her scowl. "And lots and lots of people who all loved each other very much."

Jason rolled his eyes, but his sisters and brothers were smiling. So was Caroline.

Joy's round face sagged, and she lowered her hands to her lap. "But there was one hole in their big, happy family. They didn't have a dog."

"Here we go," Joshua muttered, sinking lower in his chair.

"So they went to their good friend, Mrs. Abercromby,"

Joy continued, undaunted, "whose dog had had puppies, and they picked out the sweetest pup with big brown eyes and brought her home. And they all lived happily ever after. The end."

"We're not getting a dog, Joy," Jack said, crossing his arms over his chest.

She turned to her father. "Please, Pa? Mrs. Abercromby only has a few, and she already gave some away. We might be too late."

"Sorry, sweetheart," Mr. Willets said. "There are still too many critters that would eat it. Maybe in a few years."

Her sigh filled the room as she collapsed back beside her mother.

Caroline felt for the girl.

Mrs. Willets glanced her way. "Perhaps Caroline next?"

She pressed a hand to her chest as her heart thudded against it. Once again, all thought fled.

As if he could see she was tongue-tied, Jeremy pressed his hand on hers. "Allow me."

She nodded thankfully.

"Once, there was a cowboy named Slim," he began, leaning back in his seat and pulling his hand away in the process. She almost reached for it back, but she was still too aware of the number of people watching them.

"He lived in the dry Texas country," Jeremy explained. "He was a little on the lazy side, and he always found an excuse not to tend to his mount."

"Sounds like a few cowboys I know," Jack muttered, and Joshua avoided his look.

"The other wranglers got a might tired of always having to saddle, unsaddle, brush, feed, and water whatever horse he rode," Jeremy continued, "but they couldn't stand to see an animal suffer. So, one morning, right after a rainstorm, they saddled a pony for him. When Slim came out of the bunkhouse, he swung himself into the saddle, then glanced down.

"'Why are my feet dragging on the ground?'" he demanded.

"'Well,'" they said, "'if you leave a horse out in the rain, you can't be surprised when it shrinks.'"

Everyone started laughing, even Jack. Caroline grinned at Jeremy, who grinned back.

"I hope he learned to take care of his horse," Joy said.

"Yes, ma'am," Jeremy said. "And they all lived happily ever after. The end."

If only her story had the same ending.

That hope remained with her when Mrs. Willets declared it time for bed, and everyone headed out of the parlor. Caroline found herself beside Joy.

"Did you have a dog back in Cincinnati?" Jeremy's youngest sister asked, her voice still laced with longing.

"No," Caroline admitted. "Our house was small, and we didn't have much of a yard. But I always wanted one."

Joy sighed. "Me too." She trudged up the stairs as if all the light had left the world.

Caroline glanced down the corridor. The Willets's sons and Jane were bunched near the kitchen door, faces tight and voices murmuring, but Jeremy left with Jacob and Jane, and the others disappeared into the kitchen, so she couldn't ask why.

But something was going on, and if she was going to live here, she should do what she could to help.

CHAPTER NINE

T HE NEXT MORNING, everyone except Joanna, Jenny, Joy, and their parents looked tired at the breakfast table. Jeremy had circles under his eyes.

"We'll finish painting the one barn today," Mr. Willets said as they tucked into the griddle cakes, honey, and black cap preserves.

"Everyone except Jeremy and Caroline," his wife reminded him. "They're going riding."

Caroline had almost forgotten. A shiver went through her, but she focused on the food.

"Keep out of the forest," Jack directed from across the table.

"Thanks," Jeremy snapped. "I could have figured that out on my own."

Caroline glanced between them. Jack's brows were down in a frown. Jeremy stabbed his cake as if he thought it might escape.

"Something wrong with the forest?" their father asked.

Jeremy rallied to send his father a smile. "Always had a few too many trees for my taste."

"Besides," Jason said with a nudge to his brother Joshua, "Jeremy wants to take Caroline to the drop."

Jeremy shoved the piece of griddle cake into his mouth and didn't respond.

"What's wrong?" Caroline asked as they walked out toward the barn after breakfast. She couldn't help admiring how the freshly painted door gleamed. Of course, Jeremy looked even finer. The sunlight sent fire rippling through his hair. The cinnamon-colored duster that covered much of his shirt, trousers, and sturdy leather boots was swinging with his confident stride.

He could have fended off the question, but he answered readily enough.

"Someone's been camping in the woods," he told her, gaze going to the forest. "No real reason for concern. Jack just likes to be cautious because he's Jack. So, most of us are taking additional shifts to watch over the cattle, just in case the camper turns out to be a rustler."

He sounded more annoyed than worried, so she decided not to worry either. After all, what did she know about protecting cattle from rustlers? The whole thing sounded like something from a dime novel!

Jeremy led her to a dirt area fenced off from the barn with rails made of split logs. As he stopped beside the fence, two horses ambled over to meet him. One was already saddled and made a noise as if welcoming him. He stroked the dapple-gray nose.

"This is Quicksilver. I've had him for years. Pa generally offers each of us our own horse when we turn sixteen." He nodded to the other horse, which had a golden mane and coat with patches of white crossing the backside. "That's Calico, a very patient lady. Most of us learned to ride on her."

Was she supposed to introduce herself? She couldn't imagine curtseying to a horse, so she held out her hand. "I'm Caroline. Pleased to meet you."

Quicksilver shook his head as if she was doing it all wrong, but Calico nuzzled her hand, thick lips leaving a wet streak.

Caroline pulled back with a giggle. "That tickled. Was she saying hello?"

Jeremy patted the horse. "Calico was probably hoping for a carrot. I should have brought one. At least I had Jenny's saddle ready." He climbed the fence and moved to a rail where a blanket and leather contraption were hanging, then positioned them into place on Calico's broad back.

"There's a process to buckling and such," he said, hands working in a steady rhythm. "Don't worry about memorizing it right now. One of us will likely always be on hand to help you, but in the long run, it's wise to know how to do it yourself, just in case."

"In case of what?" she asked, watching him finish cinching various bits of leather.

"In case you and the saddle fall off," he said, stepping back.

Caroline stared at the horse's back, which was level with her eyes. "You think I might fall off from up there?"

"Everyone falls at least once," he said, returning with another set of leather strips and buckles that fit over the horse's head. "Jack fell off once a day when he was learning, Pa claimed." He winked. "Don't tell my brother I said so. He's proud of how he rides now."

Caroline nodded, trying to convince herself that the saddle wasn't as high as it looked. She'd seen ladies riding aside, but never mounting.

"How do I get up there?" she asked.

He finished with the horse's gear, then led Calico and Quicksilver out a gate to Caroline's side. His horse was definitely the taller and more powerful looking of the two.

"As Jane noted the other night, none of us lads has ever ridden sidesaddle," he acknowledged. "From what I've seen, you put foot into the stirrup and push yourself up."

It was probably easier than it sounded. He held the

horse in place with the reins. She placed her hand on his shoulder, stuck her foot into the little cup he had indicated, and straightened. Everything seemed to be going well.

Until Calico moved.

Her foot slipped, and down she went, right into Jeremy's arms.

He held her gently, smile kind. The light in his eyes warmed. So did her cheeks. She was almost disappointed when he set her upright.

"Let's try again from the mounting block," he said. "Ma and Joy use it."

He led the horse into the barn, where a little set of wooden stairs waited. He held the horse on the other side. She climbed up and managed to slide herself into the saddle.

Back home, the ladies' skirts always draped beautifully along the horse's side when they rode. Hers were all bunched up, showing her limbs nearly to her knees. Though she wiggled and tugged, she couldn't get the material down.

Jeremy's cheeks were turning red as well now. "We'll ask Ma for a riding skirt next time," he promised.

Then he showed Caroline how to use the reins. She managed to convince Calico to plod out the door of the barn and back into the sunlight.

She felt rather clever.

"Let's go a little farther," Jeremy encouraged her.

They rode out between the barns. The sky opened in all directions, blue and clear and impossibly high. A breeze ruffled the spring green of the grass. Calico's walk was slow and even, making Caroline sway forward and back.

"I rode on a boat across the Ohio River once," she told him as the horses ambled onto a track that cut through the fields. "It felt like this, rocking while you were sitting still."

"You're doing great," he assured her.

She braved herself to look toward the horizon. Beyond the trees, beyond the pastures, a massive, rugged cone of snow and rock rose in the distance, dwarfing everything around it.

"Oh, my!"

He smiled. "That's what many say the first time they see the mountain. That's Rainier. She's the biggest of the lot, the highest in all the contiguous states and territories, Jacob tells me. What I wouldn't give to stand on her top. Can you imagine the view?"

She could more easily imagine him there, standing tall and proud, buffeted by the summit winds, snow flying around him, as he gazed off across the mountain he had conquered.

"Maybe we could start with something smaller," she suggested. "Like this drop Jason keeps mentioning."

He turned away from the view, but he didn't meet her gaze. "We can ride that far when you're more comfortable."

"I feel more comfortable every moment," she promised him. "In fact, I'd like to make Calico run. Could we do that?"

He chuckled. "She's not used to running, but that's a good thing, because she's less likely to run away with you. But if you want to see what a horse can do, rein in a moment."

She did as he asked. He bent and patted Quicksilver on the shoulder, murmuring something in the alert ears. Then he straightened and shouted, "Hiya!"

The horse dove forward.

They raced away from her, dust flying up behind. Caroline put one hand to her brow to shade her eyes enough to spot them as they headed toward the horizon. A moment more, and they came thundering back, the cloud of dust parting like the Red Sea.

As she watched, heart in her throat, he threw his leg over the saddle to join the other, dropped to the ground and bounced, then came up and back into the saddle again. Such skill! Such command!

Quicksilver braced his legs as Jeremy reined in right in front of her, one hand raised in salute.

She applauded, then had to hurriedly pick up her own reins again in case she startled Calico. "Oh, Jeremy, that was famous!"

He ran his hand back over his hair, flattening it where the wind had whipped it up. "Jack and I used to try to best each other. Took me months to master that move."

"I wouldn't dare try something like that in skirts." She looked to him. "Can Jane do it?"

"When she's riding astride, maybe. But Jane doesn't like to show off." He grinned. "And I'm sure you can tell that I do."

"It's not showing off if it's displaying a hard-won talent," she told him.

"Ma might argue with you there." His smile faded as he glanced toward the barn. "Would you mind if we rode back and helped with the painting?"

"Not at all." She managed to turn Calico around, and they ambled back toward the buildings.

They spent the rest of the day scrubbing whitewash into wood, until her shoulders ached and her fingers were nearly as white as the paint. But she had to own a certain satisfaction when his father and Jack both praised her work.

They finished in time for another lively dinner.

"Caroline rode out a far piece," Jeremy reported as he passed the mashed potatoes to her. "She looked like she was born in the saddle."

She blushed under the number of admiring glances sent her way.

"And did you go to the lake or the blockhouse?" his

mother asked, lifting a few early peas on the tines of her fork. "Or the drop?"

The platter of venison wobbled in his grip as he passed it on as well. "Far enough to know Caroline will have no trouble riding. Although we need to find a riding skirt for her. Maybe one of the mercantiles in Puget City has ready-made."

His mother's eyes snapped fire. "None of my girls is wearing that shoddy ready-made. I'll make you a skirt myself, Caroline. Until it's finished, Jenny can loan you one of hers."

"Happy to oblige," Jenny assured her.

His mother went on to lay out the plans for the evening and morning. This time, she didn't give either Caroline or Jeremy a chore. Maybe that's why their steps turned for the front porch.

She felt as jittery as when she'd first mounted Calico. But he stood gazing across the dark fields into the black of the night sky, so she should probably do the same.

"There must be a million of them," Caroline said, watching the stars twinkle.

"Only about a hundred head," Jeremy said, but that teasing tone was back in his voice.

"I can see why people told stories about them," she said. "The stars, not the cows. They're so bright, like you could reach out and touch them, like they want to be part of your life."

"Can't blame the stars," Jeremy said, moving closer. "One look at you, and I want to be part of your life."

She turned to him, surprised, and his hand came up to touch her cheek, soft, reverent. Once more she closed her eyes. He was so close. Her lips puckered in anticipation.

"Are you going to kiss?"

Caroline's eyes snapped open to find Joy standing in the doorway, glancing between her and Jeremy.

"That's what courting people do, Joy," Jeremy told his sister, voice now a little sharper. "Talk, walk, kiss."

"Well, go ahead, then," she said. "But hurry up. Jack said to fetch you. It's your turn with the cows."

Jeremy shook his head. "Duty calls. Good night, Caroline." He strode into the house, leaving her wondering what might have been.

This family! At this rate, he and Caroline might manage to kiss on their thirty-fifth wedding anniversary!

Jeremy stalked down the corridor for the kitchen, nearly colliding with Jason as he came out. His younger brother held a handful of soft brown fur. "Thought you might want to give this to Caroline."

"Because nothing says love like a dead animal?" Jeremy guessed.

His brother scowled. "It's mink. I caught it in one of the traps the other day, and I skinned it. You can make something nice for her with the pelt, maybe a collar for her coat. Girls like that."

Jeremy shook his head. "And how would you know what girls like?"

"There are four of them in this family alone," Jason reminded him. "I listen. You should too."

He stalked off down the corridor, carrying the pelt with him.

Oh, he was listening. He just had more thinking to do was all.

He had plenty of time to consider as he took his turn with Jack and Jane. They'd spotted nothing unusual, but Jack still insisted on a triple guard. In the cool darkness, cattle lowing, Jeremy came to a conclusion. He couldn't do anything about his father's illness or the strangers in the woods. He *could* do something about his courtship.

"It may rain later," he told Caroline as Joshua and Joy brought in the porridge and bacon the next morning. "We should go for a ride. I want to show you the drop."

She agreed readily, but then, she didn't know what the drop meant. His brothers and sisters knew that he and Jacob had taken Deborah and Maisy there on their ill-fated visit, though not that Jeremy had made a fool of himself by proposing. When Jesse had led his Alice to see the drop on their first visit, the others had decided that's what the view was for—courting your sweetheart and giving her a kiss.

He'd almost kissed Caroline last night. She'd looked up at him so sweetly, starlight sparkling in her hair, then closed her eyes, as if she wanted to feel his lips against hers. His own longing was welling up in him again now as they rode out. He managed to keep his hands on the reins even though all he wanted was to reach out and touch her.

As they neared the edge of the cliff that ran down to the Nisqually Delta, his muscles tensed, and he slowed Quicksilver. Caroline reined in as well, easier in the saddle than he had been the first few times Pa had put him on a horse. She seemed to acclimate to new situations quickly. Another reason to admire her.

"Oh, Jeremy," she murmured, eyes shining as she gazed out over the delta. "It's beautiful."

She sounded awed. Though he'd seen the view dozens of times, he couldn't help marveling a little himself. The tide was out. The wide grasslands of the delta were greening with spring, and the Nisqually cut through them in silver braided streams, with Medicine Creek a darker gray just below. Gulls swept the skies to wheel down toward the bluer waters of Puget Sound.

He'd called Deborah lovely here, but the real beauty was sitting next to him now. The breeze fingered through

Caroline's dark hair, setting tendrils to swaying like smoke. Her lips were parted, as if she couldn't catch her breath.

"That's the Nisqually River," he told her, pointing. "That darker smudge on the far side is the cliff rising to Fort Nisqually, the old Hudson's Bay Company trading post. And there—that's a whole herd of deer."

She stared at the brown mass, which seemed to be undulating, as if they bounded across the grass for the sheer joy of it. "How marvelous! Can we ride down and see him?"

"Best not," he said with a smile. "It's not easy to get down that steep slope. You might say, it's another world there."

"A wonderful world," she assured him. "Why did you hesitate to show it to me?"

Jeremy focused on the view. "Jacob and I brought two ladies from Olympia here once. Things didn't go well."

"Why?" she asked with a frown. "Were they poor riders?"

"We never had a chance to find out. Jacob's lady decided she preferred the city, and my lady didn't care for the ranch, or me, very much."

She stuck her nose in the air. "Well, she couldn't have been very smart or very kind, then, because I think both are perfect."

She could not know how her words touched him, like liniment rubbed into a sore muscle to ease the pain.

"There's another reason I hesitated to come out this way," he admitted. "My brothers and sisters have it in their heads that this is where you bring a girl to kiss her."

"Oh."

She waited.

Expectantly.

His heart whispered a warning, but Jeremy gave in to his longings. Leaning across between the horses, he brushed his lips against hers.

They were soft and cool, but they quickly warmed. They tasted of the honey she'd put on her porridge, or maybe she was just naturally sweet. The touch of her lips, the way she sighed, the glow in her eyes as he released her were everything he could have wished for.

Jack wasn't going to get much work from him today. Such a kiss could shift the way a fellow saw the world, his future, and himself.

CHAPTER TEN

THE KISS WAS soft and sweet, a mere caress of lips, but Caroline felt it to her core. Oh the joy, the wonder! This was worth waiting for.

She opened her eyes as he pulled away. The awe on his face told her he'd felt something too.

"I guess that means you're my sweetheart," he said, smile wobbly.

She smiled back. "Guess it does."

"Just don't tell Ma," he said, turning his horse. "She'll be insufferable."

Caroline laughed, and she turned Calico as well as they headed back toward the house to offer their help with the final day of painting. She could have painted the entire barn on her own the way she was feeling. Why, she could have flown right down to that delta and introduced herself to the **deer**! She was probably still grinning when they reined in near the barn.

The others were already hard at work, but Jeremy's father gladly poured them a bucket. "Front doors need a coat too," he said, eyes twinkling.

Jacob was working on the wall on one side of the door, Jane on the other. Jeremy's brother nodded at Caroline with approval as she started slopping paint onto the planks of the door. Her shoulders protested, but she ignored them.

"How did the riding go?" Jane called.

"Caroline acquitted herself brilliantly," Jeremy said, so proudly he might have popped a button.

"We went all the way to the drop," Caroline said before thinking better of it.

Jane's eyebrows climbed. "And?"

"And there **were deer** down in the delta," Caroline said, mindful of Jeremy's warning.

"A **nice** sighting," Jacob said, but he was eyeing her as if he saw something more in her comment.

At least that nudged them away from the subject of the drop. As it was, Caroline caught Jeremy's gaze on her several times during the morning, and every time the memory of his lips against hers brought a blush to her cheeks.

She couldn't help hoping. Back home, a kiss was generally a prelude to a proposal. Maybe she'd be less mail-order and more bride soon.

Jeremy bent over their bucket and swept his brush along the sides. "We're running low."

"I'll get more," Caroline volunteered, handing him her full brush.

"I'll help you," Jacob said, abandoning his own bucket to pick up theirs.

She followed him into the barn, the scents of hay and horses wrapping around her. Jacob moved to a workbench along one wall, where the bigger vat of whitewash was waiting. They had used a good amount of it so far, but they still had a lot of barn to paint.

"You seem to have taken to riding," Jacob said as he bent to dip a smaller pail in the paint.

"It's not hard with such a gentle horse as Calico," Caroline said, watching him begin to fill her bucket. "I don't know if I'd fare as well on a bigger, faster horse like Quicksilver."

He wiped the paint off the little pail before setting it aside. "My brother's horse can be unpredictable." He straightened. "So is Jeremy, but he deserves a wife who will be steady and true. Are you that woman?"

Caroline stepped back, stung. "I've never represented myself as other than I am. Do you think I lied?"

He cocked his head as if considering, eyes half hidden behind his spectacles. "No. You appear to be honest. But do you intend to go through with this marriage if my brother proposes?"

If Jeremy proposed. So even well-read Jacob wondered.

"I came here to be a mail-order bride," Caroline said. "That hasn't changed."

"And she shouldn't have to justify that to anyone," Jack said.

Caroline turned to find him coming down the stairs from his room in the loft. He touched the brim of his hat to her, and she managed a smile.

"I was merely trying to protect Jeremy," Jacob informed his brother.

"Understandable," Jack allowed, moving to join them. "But I'm fairly sure Jeremy can protect himself. Best you head back to work."

Jacob shook his head, but he handed Caroline the bucket and stalked out.

"Sorry about that," Jack said, grabbing a hammer off the workbench. "We tend to watch out for each other."

"Which is commendable," Caroline assured him. "But I'm not out to hurt anyone."

"I can see that. You're always willing to lend a hand, and what you don't know, you're happy to learn. I hope to find a bride like you one day."

The chill she'd felt at Jacob's doubt melted. Yet, if Jeremy was right about the number of women in the area, Jack had a challenge ahead of him to find any bride at all.

"Thank you," she murmured.

He nodded as he turned for the door. "Just tell Jeremy it's time to move things along."

Maybe she should.

If she was as brave as Jeremy's oldest sister, she could ask him where she stood. Jane rode astride, like the men. Jane helped guard the cows at night. If a fellow had kissed Jane, she'd probably demand a proposal that moment. Jane might be the one proposing!

But she wasn't Jane, and pushing for anything in her family or at the academy had meant she was more likely to hear the word *no* than the word *yes*.

Caroline worked diligently beside Jeremy the rest of the afternoon, casting him the occasional glance. By the time they'd finished for the day, that glance had turned into a frown, as if she wasn't sure of him.

Why should she be sure? He'd kissed her and called her his sweetheart, which was pretty close to admitting he was hers and she was his.

But she wasn't his. Not really. Not until he uttered those fateful words: Will you marry me?

And she agreed.

As they cleaned their hands at the side of the barn before dinner, the others having gone ahead, those words trembled on his tongue, begging to be released. He'd praise her beauty, her commitment to her family, her kindness. He'd take her in his arms and press his lips against hers. They'd only had a moment at the drop. This time could be deeper, richer.

But what if he hadn't done enough to convince her to

stay? What if she agreed with Ma that they still needed time to know?

What if she said no?

What if he stopped fretting and just plunged ahead?

Beyond her, a movement caught his eye, and he blinked. Someone was heading toward the open door of the barn. He only caught a glimpse of the fellow. His hat was pulled down over his hair, but the black leather duster didn't belong to any of his brothers, and he couldn't recall seeing one on any man who attended services.

A chill went through him. He put a hand to Caroline's arm. "There's trouble. Fetch Jack. Tell him to bring his gun."

Joanna would have demanded to know what was happening. Jane would have demanded to stand with him. Caroline lifted her skirts, wide-eyed, and pelted for the house.

Jeremy drew in a breath and squared his shoulders. Was this the same fellow who'd first camped on their land? Was he armed? What did he want? Just entering the barn without permission immediately marked him as a danger. Was he after the horses? Hoping to steal equipment he could sell?

Jeremy crept up to the door. A shame he hadn't brought his revolver with him. He could do with a weapon at the moment. The only option at hand was to grab up a half-full bucket of whitewash.

The inside of the barn was dark on the best of days, with only the doors and two windows along the sides for light. They kept lanterns to a minimum because of the danger of fire. Most of the horses had been let out to pasture to graze, but he spotted Calico waiting patiently in her stall. Nothing else moved along the straw-strewn dirt floor, but something rustled in the hayloft, something that sounded a lot bigger than a mouse.

He glanced toward the house. Jack strode across the

yard, Pa puffing alongside. Both carried rifles. As they reached him, he realized Caroline was right behind them. His muscles tensed.

"Best you go back to the house," he murmured to her as she drew up alongside him. "It might not be safe out here."

"What's happened?" Jack interrupted, shifting the gun.

Jeremy had to tear his gaze away from Caroline to answer him. "A stranger entered the barn. I don't know where he came from or what he intends. I can't spot him now, but the other doors are closed, and there are noises coming from the loft."

"Cover me," Jack said.

Pa positioned himself at the side of the door, rifle trained into the barn, and Jack slipped inside.

Jeremy was more concerned with the woman standing so pale in front of him. "Please, Caroline, go back. If anything happened to you…"

From inside the barn, Jack's voice rang out. "We know you're in here. Come out now, before someone gets hurt." The sound of the rifle cocking cracked like thunder. Pa took aim.

"Don't shoot!" a voice cried. "I didn't mean any trouble."

Caroline's eyes widened once more. She shoved past Jeremy. He whirled to stop her, heart leaping into his throat, but she ran into the barn.

"Don't shoot!" she cried, echoing the stranger. "That's my brother!"

She could hardly believe her ears, and yet, there was Ned, clambering down the ladder from the hayloft. She ran and threw her arms around him. Was he thinner? His face more worn?

He certainly smelled of the saddle and dusty roads. It was all she could do not to wrinkle her nose as she released him.

"Are you all right?" she asked. "Where have you been?"

He took off his low-brimmed hat with one hand and rubbed the back of his neck with the other. His honey-colored hair hung limp around his face. "Sorry to worry you. I had to go away on urgent business. As soon as I got back, I went straight to the lodging house. I read the note you'd left with Mrs. Potts, and I lit out for Washington Territory to find you."

Away on business? He and his friends were more likely to be found gambling with dice behind the house.

A dozen questions crowded her tongue, but he clearly didn't want to elaborate in front of an audience. His gaze kept darting around as if he wondered which of the men was going to open fire first.

She patted his shoulder, raising a puff of dust, then turned to smile at Jeremy, his father, and his brother. Jack had his eyes narrowed and gun still trained on her brother. Mr. Willets had at least lowered his rifle. And Jeremy was watching, tense and coiled, as if ready to jump in and rescue her at the least provocation.

"I'm sorry he scared everyone," she said. "Mr. Willets, Jack, Jeremy, this is my brother, Ned Cadhill."

Ned nodded respectfully. "Sirs."

Jeremy's father nodded back. "Pleased to make your acquaintance, son."

Jack said nothing, but he lowered his rifle too.

Jeremy came forward and offered his hand. "I'm Jeremy."

Ned took his hand and pumped. Hard. "So, you're the man who took my sister away."

Caroline drew herself up as the two disengaged. "Don't you go blaming Jeremy. *I* took myself away, after *you* left!"

His easy grin popped into view. "I was just teasing, sis. Though you could have told me you were planning to be a mail-order bride before you left that note." He nodded around again. "Glad to meet you all. Thank you for taking care of Caroline when I couldn't."

"Your sister is a breath of spring and a blessing to everyone she meets," Jeremy's father said, his words bringing heat to her cheeks. "Dinner should be on the table shortly. You're welcome to stay."

Jeremy's father led Jack from the barn.

"I have a horse in the woods," Ned said with an apologetic look to Jeremy. "I don't suppose I could use a stall?"

"Use whatever you need," Jeremy said. "You heard my father. Any family of Caroline's is welcome here."

"I'll join you all shortly, then," he said.

Caroline broke away from Jeremy to face her brother squarely. "And don't you think of leaving again! This time, I'll have help to track you down!"

He grimaced. "I'm not going anywhere."

"Good." She took Jeremy's arm and let him escort her from the barn.

"Remind me never to get on your bad side," he said as they headed for the house. "Then again, I didn't know you had a bad side."

Out of the corner of her eye, she saw her brother making for the trees across the field.

"I suppose everyone has a bad side," she said as Jeremy held the kitchen door open for her. "It just takes more to bring it out in some. And Ned is very good at bringing mine out."

"Is that why you didn't tell him about answering my ad?" he asked.

She stepped into the warmth of the house with a sigh. "No. I didn't tell my father either. They both seemed to think it was fine for me to stay as I was, keeping house for them. I wanted something of my own, someone who would want me for me."

There, she'd confessed it. She slanted him a glance.

In answer, he stepped closer, breath brushing her cheek. "Nothing wrong with that. I've wanted the same. Sometimes, I think our families don't really know us or at least appreciate us for who we are."

"That's it exactly," she said with a sigh.

His hand came up to stroke her hair, and she wanted to lean into the touch. "I see you, Caroline. You're sweet and helpful and you look for the best in every situation. You make me want to be the best."

"As far as I'm concerned," she murmured, feeling as if he'd reached down to touch her heart as well, "you *are* the best."

He lowered his head. "No, I'm not. If I was, I'd be questioning your brother instead of mooning over you."

She didn't mind the mooning one bit, but his reminder brought the world crashing back in. Whatever her concerns about a future with this man, she had to deal with her brother first.

"Don't worry," she told Jeremy, starting down the corridor for the dining room. "As soon as I have a chance, I'm going to ask questions until I'm satisfied."

She didn't have an opportunity as everyone gathered for dinner. Mr. Willets must have had a word with his wife, because another chair had been added to the table as if in expectation of Ned joining them.

He came in just as the others were seating themselves, setting a battered valise dirtier than his clothes inside the dining room door. He'd removed the travel-worn duster, and he must have dunked his head in a water barrel, because his hair was damp and slicked back from his now-clean face. Still, the hint of stubble along his jaw made him look more like an outlaw than a caller.

Caroline hurried to introduce him to the rest of Jeremy's family. He nodded to Jacob, Jason, and Joshua and bowed to Jane and Jenny. He winked at Joy. But he smiled at Joanna as he was seated next to her across the table from Caroline and Jeremy.

"I see they spoke the truth when they said the West boasted a number of prairie roses," he said.

"You apparently missed the stories about thistle and tumbleweed," Joanna countered. But she swiped a stray curl back into place before passing him the bowl of potatoes.

"It must have been a long ride from Cincinnati," Mrs. Willets said as she kept the platters of ham and biscuits moving. "What roads did you take, Mr. Cadhill?"

"Whichever led West," he joked. "These have to be the finest rhubarb preserves I've ever eaten, Mrs. Willets. You'll have to give Caroline the recipe."

Apparently he thought she'd still be doing his cooking. She sliced into her piece of ham hard enough that the knife squeaked on the porcelain.

"Why, Caroline is an excellent cook in her own right," Jeremy's mother said with a fond smile her way. "She made us the most delicious pie just the other night. But your brother is right, dear. We should exchange more recipes."

Caroline hastily swallowed. "I never wrote anything down. I just did what I'd seen my mother do. No one ever complained." They hadn't praised the food either, but she hadn't expected them to. She'd just enjoyed cooking, trying new things, and feeling like she was doing her part to support her father and Ned.

"No reason to complain," Ned put in. "Caroline succeeds at everything she sets her hand to. I'm sure you all noticed."

They all nodded and beamed, as if she were the best thing that had ever happened to them. Warmth seeped into her, and she dropped her gaze to her plate.

Her brother was being very nice, but he wasn't fooling her. She couldn't wait to get him alone and learn the truth about why he'd left and why he'd returned.

CHAPTER ELEVEN

JEREMY SAT ACROSS from Caroline's brother, watching as Ned teased Joanna on one side and joked with Joshua on the other. Was his own teasing that annoying? Or did Ned's voice have a desperate edge to it?

Why would Caroline's brother have been hiding in the woods? Who else had been with him? Why had he left Caroline behind in Cincinnati in the first place? Hadn't he realized she would worry? He should have been there to protect her, to provide for her. Had he come to his senses, or was there another reason for his sudden appearance now?

"I hope you concluded your business to your satisfaction, Ned," he said when he could get a word in. "It must have been powerful urgent to force you away from your sister."

Ma shot him a look, but she took a bite of her potatoes as if to keep from scolding Jeremy. She had to be just as eager for answers from the newcomer among them.

"The matter seems to be settled," Ned allowed. "Which is why I felt comfortable hastening to my sister's side. And here I find her, surrounded by friends."

"And what are your plans now?" Jeremy pressed.

He leaned back in his chair and spread his arms, which

put one of them dangerously close to draping about Joanna's shoulders. As if she noticed too, his sister blushed. Jeremy tried not to bristle, but Jack stiffened.

"Why, I'm here for a wedding, aren't I?" Ned asked, looking around as if for confirmation. "Although, I find it odd. My sister came all this way to be a bride, yet I don't see a ring on her finger." His gaze came back to Jeremy's and held.

"Jeremy and I are becoming better acquainted," Caroline explained. "It's lovely to be part of a true courtship after only having his letters to go by."

Guilt nipped. His sisters expected picnics and what not. Caroline had been given barn painting. She had every right to a proposal, but he couldn't blame her brother's appearance for his lack of courage today.

"We all want what's best for Caroline and Jeremy," his mother said. "I think there's a little more of the preserves left. Jane, would you pass them and the biscuits to Mr. Cadhill, since he enjoyed them so much?"

Ned drew in his arms and held up one hand as if to forestall Jane. "Thank you, but I couldn't eat another bite."

"You'll want some of the ginger cake for dessert, I'm sure," Ma said. "Joanna baked it."

Joanna cast him a glance under her lashes.

"Well then," he said with a grin to her, "I'll make room."

Joanna excused herself to fetch the cake.

Ma steered the conversation for the rest of the meal, laying out her orders for the evening and morning, then herded Ned and Caroline into the parlor. He made sure to carry his valise with him as if he wondered whether she was going to let him stay the night. Ma likely thought she could question their visitor more effectively without the rest of them listening. She had had years of experience squeezing information out of Jeremy and his siblings.

Jack must have had his suspicions as well, for he intercepted Jeremy before he could follow.

"Do you think Ned could be our mystery camper?" he asked as Jason, Jenny, and Joy began clearing the table. Joanna was supposed to be helping too, but she'd positioned herself in the doorway as if to overhear what was happening in the parlor across the hall.

"I've wondered," Jeremy admitted. "But if he was, why wait in the woods or Puget City? And who did he have with him? Maybe Ned really did arrive at the Jumping J this afternoon."

Jack wiggled his jaw as if chewing on the matter. "How much do you know about him?

"Only what Caroline wrote me and what she's mentioned since she came," Jeremy said. "He lived like a rich man's son, never finding a profession or looking for work, even though his father was only a bank clerk."

Jack snorted. "Or a gentleman thief, according to Joy."

He glanced to where his littlest sister was rolling up the tablecloth for washing, then drew Jack farther away from the table and Joanna.

"Caroline thinks he's innocent. The bank took her home and all their savings to recoup the loss, and she moved into lodgings. Then Ned disappeared, and someone came to the rooming house, threatening to harm her if she didn't tell them where he'd gone. As she had no idea and no one to protect her, she lit out."

Jack's lips thinned. "Could her brother have been involved in the theft? Perhaps he was the one who stole the money, and their father allowed himself to be blamed to protect him."

Jeremy shook his head. "Ned couldn't be directly involved. He'd have had no opportunity to steal the money. Caroline thinks someone else took the cash and blamed it on her father."

"I don't like it," Jack said, rubbing his chin with the back of one hand. "If Ned Cadhill is the thief, we'll need to watch him. If he isn't, and the real thief is still looking for him, we'll need to be ready to defend the family."

And Caroline.

Normally Caroline enjoyed any time she spent with the family, but tonight she was aware of too many competing concerns. First, Mrs. Willets had cornered her and Ned in the parlor while the others either cleaned up from supper or, in the case of Mr. Willets, Jacob, and Jane, headed off to tend the cows.

"What is it you did in Cincinnati, Mr. Cadhill?" Jeremy's mother asked from her spot on the sofa as Caroline sat on a nearby chair and Ned strolled back and forth in front of his valise.

He paused to bow. "You might say I'm a gentleman of leisure, ma'am."

As Mrs. Willets frowned, Caroline felt compelled to explain. "Ned had a tutor for a while, and he did very well in his studies, never a complaint against him. I imagine he could do whatever he wanted."

Her brother eyed her as he continued his perambulations. "Why, thank you, sis."

"Commendable, to be sure," Mrs. Willets agreed. "And are you planning to return to the city or stay out West?"

"I have yet to decide." He moved to the bookcase and tilted his head as if reading the gilded titles on the spines. "Cincinnati was always home, but I find much to admire in this new country."

Joanna popped into the room, and he straightened to grin at her.

"Done," she said somewhat breathlessly as Jenny followed her into the parlor. "May we do something for entertainment tonight, Ma, seeing as how we have a guest?"

If Mrs. Willets was dismayed to find her questioning interrupted, she didn't show it as the rest of the family who weren't on duty outside streamed into the room. Joanna sat next to her mother, and Ned came to light on the arm of the sofa beside her. Jenny, Joy, Jason, and Joshua found seats around the room. Jeremy settled on the chair closest to Caroline's, but she caught him watching her brother as if waiting for him to do something tremendously marvelous.

Or tremendously wicked.

"What about I Spy?" Jenny suggested.

Joy clapped her hands. "Yes, please! Caroline can go first."

Caroline and Ned had played the game, so she knew the rules, but she demurred. "Someone else can take the first turn. I enjoy the guessing more."

Ned nudged Joanna with his elbow. "Perhaps Joanna should take the first turn. I warrant she has a clever imagination."

"Clever enough to recognize when someone is trying to dump the butter boat over my head," she told him, but her eyes were bright.

"Go ahead, Joanna," their mother said. "Show Mr. Cadhill how it's done."

Joanna inclined her head, then glanced around the room. Sitting up tall and staring straight ahead, she announced, "I spy with my little eye something red."

Immediately everyone began looking around.

Jeremy laughed. "There are six red-heads in this room alone. It could be any of them."

Joanna rolled her eyes. "Something red that isn't hair, then.

Joy pointed to the bookcase. "That book!"

Her sister shook her head, smile hovering.

"Is it square?" Joshua asked.

"No," Joanna allowed.

"Is it round?" Jason challenged.

She grinned. "Yes."

"Is it even in this room?" Jason demanded.

Joanna cast a quick glance at Ned. "Oh, yes."

Caroline focused on her brother. Neither his shirt nor his trousers was red. His brow puckered as if he couldn't figure it out either.

Joy pointed. "Mr. Cadhill's cheeks! They're turning red!"

They were indeed, for all he tried to look away.

Joanna laughed. "Well done, Joy! Yes, I was spying Mr. Cadhill's cheeks, which I knew would turn red when he realized I'd bested him."

He inclined his head, cheeks blazing. "Your point, Miss Willets."

"You'll get tired of the Miss Willets and Mr. Willets business," Joshua predicted. "There are simply too many of us."

"You're nearly family," Jenny agreed. "He can use our first names, can't he, Ma?"

Mrs. Willets considered him a moment before nodding. "It would likely be easier, Mr. Cadhill."

"Well, then, you must call me Ned," he said. "And we can dispense with all the miss and misters, except for our patriarch and his charming wife, of course."

He was the one being charming. Wait until she got him alone!

They played a few more rounds, and her brother was his usual self, teasing and laughing, but every once in a while, he'd peer out the front window, as if he expected someone to peer back.

Finally, Caroline guessed one of the items, which made it her turn to give them a riddle. She thought for a moment. Many of the distinguishable items in the room had already been used. But then, no one had said it had to be in the room or even in the house.

"I spy with my little eye," she said, careful not to look out the window, "something big."

"Bigger than the barn?" Joshua immediately asked.

Caroline shook her head. "No."

"Bigger than a **herd of deer**?" Jeremy asked with a wink.

"No," she admitted, smiling.

"Bigger than a cow?" Joy asked.

"No," she said.

"What about a horse?" Jenny put in.

That was harder. She couldn't really answer the question yes or no as the game required. She bit her lip a moment, then noticed Jeremy had fixed on her face and she had to look away. "The same size as a horse."

"*Is* it a horse?" Joy suggested.

"Not *a* horse," Caroline hazarded. "A *specific* horse."

"Quicksilver," Joshua guessed. "He's the fastest."

Caroline shook her head.

"Calico," Jeremy said. "You like her."

She beamed at him. "Well, you introduced us."

"Because I knew you'd like her. You make a mighty fine rider, even when you have to hike up your skirts."

"Ahem," Ma said as the others tittered, and Caroline laughed. "I believe you won that round, Jeremy. What do you spy? And it better not be anyone's skirts."

"I spy with my little eye," he said, gazing at Caroline, "the prettiest gal in the whole territory."

"Joanna!" Ned crowed, and Joanna stared at him.

"No," Jeremy said, keeping his gaze on Caroline. "And if you can't guess right, you haven't been watching me closely enough." He took her hand and pressed a kiss against her knuckles.

She couldn't breathe, couldn't speak. Didn't want to move.

"Caroline Cadhill," his mother said, and Caroline sucked in a breath until she saw the smile on Mrs. Willets's face.

Her name had just been a guess, not a scold. In fact, Mrs. Willets looked pleased beyond all measure as she rose.

"Now, it's past time for bed. Jenny, Joshua, and Joy remember that you're helping in the kitchen tomorrow morning, so I expect you down before the rooster crows."

Joshua heaved a sigh but nodded and went to peck her on the cheek. The others took turns bidding their mother goodnight.

Jeremy stayed with Caroline, leaning closer until she caught the scent of spice that must be from his shaving soap. "Will you be all right?" He glanced to where Ned was waiting by the parlor door, watching Joanna.

"Fine," she promised him. "And I hope to have something more to tell you in the morning."

He reached out and gave her hand a squeeze before going to kiss his mother. Much as she enjoyed his touch, she could not help noticing that her brother and Joanna had their heads entirely too close together.

"Ned," Mrs. Willets called as if she'd noticed it too, and Ned's head snapped up.

"Ma'am?" His voice had a squeak to it.

"I've put you in with your sister," she explained. "Please let me know if you need anything."

"You've already given me far more than I deserve," Ned assured her with an expansive bow. "Good food, good companionship." His gaze lingered on Joanna as she left the room with Joy. He forced his gaze back to their hostess. "I am forever in your debt."

"Nonsense," she said. "If you owe me a debt, it is only the same one I owe you—the responsibility of Christians to help one another."

Something crossed his face, but he offered her a smile. He picked up his valise, and Caroline was finally able to get him out of the parlor and all to herself.

She led him up the stairs and into the room at the

top. Then she shut the door and leaned against it. If he wanted to escape her questioning this time, he'd either have to move her or climb out the window.

"All right, Ned," she said, crossing her arms over her chest. "Explain yourself. You didn't have any business that forced you out of town. Why did you leave then, and why are you here now?"

He sighed as he sank onto the nearest bed and set the valise carefully beside it. "You know me too well, sis. I ran for the same reason you did. I was out with friends, and three men approached me. They demanded that I hand over Father's money, and they promised they'd make you pay if I didn't."

Her arms dropped. "Oh, Ned. No!"

He started tugging at a boot, steadfastly avoiding her gaze. "Well, I couldn't give them the money, could I?" The first boot fell with a thud, and he went to work on the other. "I thought that if I left, they'd either follow me or give up, and you'd be safe."

She pushed off the door. "But I wasn't safe. They came to the house too, as I said in my note, only they claimed to be looking for you."

He set the other boot down with its twin, then rose and padded toward her in his stockinged feet. "I got to worrying that that might happen, so I came back to Cincinnati to check on you. I'm so sorry, Caroline." He wrapped his arms around her and held her.

Poor fellow! He'd probably been as frightened as she had been. And he'd obviously ridden far. Why, she'd spotted that big toe sticking out of one stocking.

He pulled back and smiled at her. "At least you landed somewhere safe. Your intended's family seems very nice."

"The nicest," she assured him as he padded back to the bed. "Why did you think you had to sneak in and hide in the barn?"

He grimaced. "Well, I wasn't sure about them then.

That Jeremy could have been leading you on. I wanted to see you first, find out if you liked it here."

"I like it just fine," she said. "And I'm hoping for a proposal soon." At least she could say that to her brother!

Ned pulled back the covers. "Do you think they'd let me stay? I'd be glad for the work, but I know I have a lot to learn."

"I'm sure they'd be happy to help you get back on your feet," Caroline said. "And so would I."

"Thanks. I could always count on you." He waited, and she turned her back so he could remove his clothing. When the bedclothes rustled again, she waited until he'd rolled away from her before undoing the buttons on her bodice.

Her father in prison, her brother in hiding, all because someone had been greedy. If Ned hadn't come back to read her note, she might never have seen him again.

She blinked, fingers frozen on the last button. Ned had said the men had come to him looking for their father's supposed stolen funds. But they hadn't asked her for the money. They'd asked her about Ned. She reviewed their conversation again, but she didn't think she'd misheard.

"Ned?" she asked, moving closer to his bed. "Why would those men think you had the bank's money?"

A snore rumbled up from her brother's prone form.

How convenient.

Jeremy hung around the top of the stairs the next morning. He wanted to hear what Caroline had learned from her brother, but more, he wanted to see her, to touch her, to assure himself she hadn't fared ill by Ned's coming. He'd thought about their kiss and his next steps most of the night. After Deborah, he'd been ready to marry for companionship, but so much had changed since he'd placed that ad and read Caroline's answer. He'd come to care, likely more than was wise. Was it fair to bring her into the family when he wasn't sure about the danger or his father's health?

Was he cheating her by keeping her from finding a true love?

"You're not helping in the kitchen this morning," Jenny said, pausing beside him. "And you aren't supposed to be milking or watching the cows. Why are you up so early?"

"Same reason Joanna is," Jane grumbled, stifling a yawn as she passed for the stairs. "They want to see their sweethearts."

"I don't have a sweetheart," Joanna informed her tartly. She held up a brush. "Caroline and I are going to help each other with our hair, just like we did for church."

He would have believed her, if his sister's hair hadn't already been brushed and pulled away from her face with her best tortoiseshell combs to spill down behind her in a cascade of crimson curls.

"I'll just see if they're up," Jeremy said. He tapped at the door and heard a muffled, "Come in."

Easing open the door, he found that Caroline was awake and dressed in the blue gingham gown she'd worn when she arrived, with her own dark hair bound in a braid around her head. Joanna must have been standing on tiptoe, for he felt her attempting to peer over his shoulder.

Caroline prodded the bundle of blankets in Jacob's old bed with one finger. "Breakfast, Ned. Downstairs. A quarter hour. No more."

The bundle squirmed, and a few harsh words shot out.

Joanna fell onto her soles with a gasp.

Ned threw back the covers and sat up to stare, first at Jeremy, and likely the skirts behind his legs, and then at Caroline. "Why didn't you tell me we had company?"

"It's not our house," Caroline informed him, marching

past him. "*We* are the company here. Mind your manners, and get up."

She swept out the door and shut it behind her.

"Apologies," she said to Jeremy and Joanna, whose cheeks were nearly the same shade as her hair. "He's never coherent until he's had breakfast. Mother used to say he needed a little sugar to sweeten his disposition."

Ma would have said Ned needed a good talking to instead. But Caroline's brother was a man grown, if barely. It was time he sorted things out for himself and stopped making his sister carry his weight.

As Joanna hurried to return the brush to her room, Jeremy led Caroline down the stairs. He peered in the dining room, but no one was at the table yet, the others likely busy with one task or another.

"Did he explain himself to you?" he asked, studying her face. He couldn't help thinking that the dark smudges under her warm eyes were her brother's fault.

"Not really," Caroline admitted. She ran a hand up her arm. "He says men threatened my safety unless he turned over the money my father supposedly stole. He thought if he left town, the threats would stop."

Jeremy snorted. "He should have realized they'd just transfer the threats to you."

"I know," she said with a sigh that cracked his heart.

She shouldn't have to bear this burden alone. "I could talk to him," Jeremy offered.

He hadn't realized one of his hands had fisted until she took it in her own. "You will never know how much it means that you want to help. Thank you. But I can handle Ned."

Much as he longed to fight her battles, he had to take her at her word.

And hope.

CHAPTER TWELVE

NED CAME DOWN as the last of the family was seated. Jeremy noticed that he hadn't taken the time to shave, and golden stubble speckled his chin and cheeks. He wore the same clothes from the day before too, as if he hadn't bothered to pull another set from his valise. Then again, maybe he'd escaped Cincinnati with whatever he had had on hand.

They all set in to the porridge and sourdough toast with peach preserves after Pa had said the blessing, though Caroline watched her brother as closely as Jeremy did.

"Was the bed to your liking, Ned?" Ma asked as she buttered her toast.

"Never slept so soundly in my life, ma'am," he told her, accepting the preserves Joanna offered him. Their fingers brushed, and she blushed.

So did Ned.

Jeremy caught Jack's look from near the top of the table. His brother had seen the exchange too. Funny. They both understood that their sisters would fall in love someday. But Jeremy had never realized until that moment how few men could be worthy of them.

"I'm glad to hear it," Ma said to Ned before turning to her youngest son. "Joshua, you can help your father this morning as we planned, but I've decided to spare you from your lessons this afternoon. Mrs. Abercromby and I are organizing an auction after Easter to help raise money for the new church. Take two of my quilts to her, and then deliver her inventory of the items she's received so far to Reverend Dalrymple."

"Two quilts, very generous," Pa said, porridge on his spoon. "I know a few fellows who would gladly bid on those."

"New church?" Ned asked, glancing around.

"We don't have a church building," Jane told him. "One of the local farmers intends to move on, and he offered to sell our minister the house and land if he could raise sufficient funds in time."

"That's the greatest obstacle," Pa added. "Time. Henshaw wants to move on by June. I don't know if we can raise the money before then, even the low amount he agreed as the price."

Jenny looked across the table. "Maybe Caroline and I can bake some pies. Those always go over well."

"I'd be happy to help," Caroline said. "And those apple preserves might make good cobblers."

"Let's talk after breakfast," Jenny said.

"And I'll talk with Mr. Dalrymple on Sunday," Jack added. "Maybe there's something the boys and I can offer that he could auction."

"Strong backs and burly shoulders?" Jane teased him.

Jacob adjusted his spectacles. "I certainly hope we can offer more than that."

"A great deal more," Pa assured him. "And all of it is wanted today to finish the painting."

A chorus of groans rose.

"Maybe I could help with that," Ned said as the sound faded.

Jack's eyes narrowed, but Pa nodded. "I'll take you up on that offer."

Caroline puffed out a sigh. Jeremy thought he knew

why. The busier her brother kept, the less opportunity she'd have to quiz him.

But the more opportunity he and Jack would have to watch him.

What a delight to use her cooking skills for such a good cause! Caroline and Jenny did their own inventory of the family's baking supplies while Jane and Joy finished washing and putting away the breakfast dishes.

"Enough supplies for two apple cobblers, three rhubarb pies, and four dozen gingersnaps," Jenny said, stepping back. "That's a lot of cooking, Miss Cadhill."

"It is indeed, Miss Willets," Caroline said with a grin. "But I think we're up to it."

Joy turned from the big porcelain sink, drying a plate. "Can I help?"

"Of course," Jenny said. "But this time, listen to what I say about the salt."

Joy nodded, curls bobbing. "I will. I promise! And Caroline, I know just what you should do about your wedding."

Caroline blinked. Was Jeremy's youngest sister offering to intercede in their courtship? She looked so eager, smile lighting her round face, that Caroline didn't have the heart to tell her she and Jeremy must figure that out on their own.

"Oh?" she said instead.

Joy set the plate and towel aside and hurried forward. "Yes. We should hold it in the pasture, when all the wildflowers are blooming."

Jane turned from the washing, hands covered in suds. "There are a few things in the pasture besides the wildflowers, Joy. Like cows and what they leave behind."

Joy ignored her, clearly warming to her theme. Her

hands were clasped in front of her again, as if she were about to give a great oration. "It must be a sunny day, so the light shines on your hair. And I can weave a crown from wildflowers to cover your veil. You'll look like a princess!"

"If she's wearing a veil, the sunlight isn't going to shine on her hair," Jenny pointed out. "Maybe we should wait until the new church is built."

Joy sighed, deflating. "Oh, I suppose."

"It was a lovely idea," Caroline assured her. "And if Jeremy and I get married when the wildflowers are blooming, there is no one else I would trust to make me a crown."

She brightened again. "I can't wait."

Neither could Caroline.

They finished in the kitchen a short time later, and Caroline and Jenny carried out water and cups for the painters. Caroline was glad for the chance to see Jeremy and to check on her brother. Mr. Willets had apparently paired Ned with Jack to take on the big wall to the left of the door Caroline and Jeremy had painted. Her brother seemed to be stroking on the paint as carefully as Jack did, even though he'd never painted anything before.

"Pies planned?" Jeremy asked as she poured him a cup of water.

"Pies, cobblers, and cookies," she answered. She leaned closer and lowered her voice. "How's Ned been behaving?"

"Like a tenderfoot," Jeremy confided. "He has no experience, but at least he seems eager to learn."

They might have said the same of her. She continued to watch her brother as they all took a break for water. He joked with each of Jeremy's siblings, setting Joanna to blushing again. He even climbed into the loft to examine Joshua's work on the upper part of the barn and praised him for it before falling into a conversation with the youngest lad. Joshua headed off to see Mrs. Abercromby and the minister a short while later with a pleased smile on his face.

"You have anything else you want done, Mr. Willets?" Ned asked Jeremy's father, pausing to wipe a drop of water off his mouth with the back of his hand as they all prepared to resume work. Jenny collected the empty pitchers and cups to take to the house, and Caroline donned an apron to help with the painting.

"Tired of painting already?" Mr. Willets asked her brother with an amused look.

"No, sir. I could probably paint for hours yet." He stretched as if to prove it, and Jason snorted. "I just wanted to make sure you knew I was here to help."

"Glad to hear it, son," Jeremy's father said. "Jack knows more about what needs doing these days. I'm sure he could find a use for you."

Jack had taken a drink of water, and it must have gone down wrong, for he choked, and Jane had to pat him on the back.

"Let's finish the barn," he said when he could speak. "We can discuss other tasks later."

"Rain's supposed to come in tomorrow afternoon," Jacob offered with a look to the puffy clouds in the sky. "Best to get the whitewash on today so it has a little chance to dry."

"I can stay and help," Jason volunteered. "I was supposed to pick up some pins and thread for Ma, but that can wait a day."

Ned perked up. "I could get those for you. On my horse, Puget City's only a short jaunt."

Interesting. If her brother had ridden straight here, how had he known the distance to Puget City? Or had he stopped there first to ask directions? She'd certainly needed help to find the Jumping J.

Of course, leaving the ranch for at least part of the

afternoon meant she would have no more opportunity to question him.

So she followed him into the barn as he went to saddle his horse. Coming in from the light, the shadows gathered closer along with the familiar musty scents. Ned was standing by a dainty black horse with soulful eyes, whose head bobbed. He reached out a hand.

"Where'd you get her?" Caroline asked, peering over the top of the stall.

Ned started as if he hadn't realized she was there, then busied himself with the blanket and saddle. "I bought her off a man who had moved to Cincinnati and didn't have a place for her anymore." He smiled as he ran a hand down her shoulder. "Maria's been a faithful friend."

He sounded so happy, she almost didn't ask, but she had to know. "Why did those men come to you asking about the bank's money?"

He kept cinching and buckling, his actions not nearly as smooth as Jeremy's. But then, Jeremy had been doing it his whole life. "They thought Father was guilty. No one ever found the money, so they assumed he'd given it to me."

Of course they had. She should have realized that. "Well, we're shed of them now. I don't see how they could find us here."

He shot her a grin. "The blessings of living in the wilderness."

Blessings indeed. The work here was unending, but so was the camaraderie. Her father had toiled for years with little to show for it. Jeremy's family grew and raised what they needed, and they still helped others. And every day, the land changed with the seasons. Now it was ripening with spring. What would it be like in summer? Fall? Winter?

"How did you find the Jumping J?" she asked as he led Maria out of the stall.

He frowned at her. "The Jumping J?"

"That's what Joy named the ranch," she explained. "Were you here earlier, camping in the woods to make sure you had the right ranch?"

"No," he said, lower lip out as if he wondered why she'd ask. "Your note said you were going to stay with the Willets family near Puget City, Washington Territory. I went there and asked, and someone pointed me in this direction."

Very much like how she'd found the place, only she'd asked in Olympia.

"Well, I'm glad you're here," Caroline said, walking with him toward the barn door. "Maybe we've both found a home."

"You're going to marry him, then?" he asked, pausing just inside the shadows.

Caroline raised her chin. "If we decide we suit."

"You still trying to figure that out?" Ned shook his head. "I can tell within minutes whether a gal is going to suit me or not." He swung up into the saddle. "I'll be back in time for dinner." He clucked to Maria and rode off.

Minutes to know whether to marry a person? An important decision like that shouldn't be made on an impulse! Then again, Jeremy's parents had fallen in love at first sight, and they seemed very happy together.

She and Jeremy just needed to find some middle ground!

He edged closer to her as she went to retrieve a brush to help him. "Any luck with Ned?"

"He has an answer for every question," she allowed, smacking her brush against the wood.

Jeremy stepped back as if to avoid the spray. "Answers you can live with?"

"For the most part," she said. "I don't think he was your camper, Jeremy. I know that doesn't help much."

"More than you might think," Jack said from farther down the wall, proving he had been listening to every word.

Jeremy frowned at him, but his brother moved to join them. "Jason saw someone at the edge of the forest this morning while he was watching the cows. When he rode closer, the fellow disappeared into the woods."

"Tell me he was smart enough not to go after him alone," Jeremy demanded.

"He didn't," Jack assured him. "But it's all the more reason to think this has nothing to do with Caroline's brother and more to do with rustlers."

Jeremy held up his brush like a sword. "You are not doubling the watch again. We don't have any sisters or brothers left!"

"Could I help?" Caroline asked, glancing between them.

"No," Jeremy said, dropping his brush into the bucket. "It's not safe."

"But if Jane can ride watch…" she started.

"Jane has been riding watch since she was twelve," Jeremy told her, face hard. "Jane can shoot a knot out of a plank of wood at twenty paces."

His words stung. Just when she was fitting in, it seemed she wasn't. Back in Cincinnati, it had been her lack of wealth and connections that held her back. Here, it appeared to be her ability to ride a horse and shoot a gun!

Jack put a hand on Caroline's shoulder, but his gaze was on Jeremy. "No one expects you to ride or shoot like Jane, Caroline. Even Joanna and Jenny can't match her there. But we need experienced folks to watch the cows if there are rustlers in the area. You help in other ways. That's good enough for me. What about you, brother?"

Of course it was good enough for him. He'd already decided Caroline might be a little *too* good for him. It wasn't a matter of ability. It was a matter of safety. The idea of putting her in danger knotted his gut.

"Caroline's proven she's an asset to any family she cares to join," he told them both. "But cooking is a lot safer than riding herd."

"Then perhaps I should just stay in the kitchen," she said. She dropped her brush in the bucket and headed for the kitchen door, head down and skirts swishing in her hurry.

"You hurt her feelings," Jack said, watching her.

"Because you know so much about feelings," Jeremy retorted, ache growing inside.

"I know pain when I see it," he countered. "You want to marry that gal, best you talk to her about it."

He wasn't sure how, but he had to try. He took only long enough to wipe the whitewash from his fingers with a turpentine-soaked rag, then strode after Caroline.

Ma glanced up from checking the venison roast as he came through the kitchen, the rich scent filling the air. She shut the oven door and straightened. "What did you do?"

"Something I'm going to apologize for," he said, heading for the corridor. He was just thankful his mother didn't follow him.

He found Caroline on the front porch, curled up on one of the chairs. She avoided his gaze as he came to take the chair beside hers.

"I didn't mean to hurt you," he said. "I didn't agree with Jack at first that these strangers were rustlers, but I'm coming around to the idea. Rustlers aren't nice people, Caroline. Sometimes, when they try to take a herd, people get shot, trampled, killed."

She flinched. "Then we should send for the police."

"We don't have a police force," he told her. "We have a sheriff and a few deputies for all of Thurston County. We can't send for them until we know what we're dealing with, and we won't know what we're dealing with until someone strikes." He reached out a hand and rested it on hers. "If something should happen to you, I'd never forgive myself."

"I took care of myself, mostly, in Cincinnati," she said softly.

"You must have faced things in the city I'll never face here," he agreed. "But I doubt you had to worry about bears wandering into the yard, a cougar going after a calf, or rustlers trying to steal your livelihood."

She sighed. "No, only thieves at the bank sending my father to prison."

He squeezed her hand. "That's bad enough. I just don't want you to have come all this way only to meet something worse. Won't you let me protect you?"

"Of course," she said readily, but she still didn't look at him. She'd had too many examples of men who hadn't fulfilled their vows of protection. He couldn't blame her for doubting his.

"I'm sorry if I made it sound as if I expected you to stay inside at all times," he tried again. "I thought that was how you'd lived in Cincinnati, and I got the impression from your letters that you liked cooking and cleaning."

She regarded him. "I'm not sure anyone *enjoys* cleaning, although I will own to a certain satisfaction when I see things tidy and sparkling. And I do enjoy cooking. Back home, it was a challenge to find the best foods on our budget. But here?" She waved a hand at the fields. "You have a bounty in easy reach!"

"Not necessarily easy," Jeremy said, leaning back in the

chair. "Things are already starting to grow, so you haven't seen the worst of winter. We slaughter a few pigs, maybe a sheep, and a cow or two every fall and smoke the meat or make sausages or jerky. Ma puts up fruit and vegetable preserves. But meals get a little thin around January when it's hard to hunt in the cold and nothing much is growing. Someone else who knows how to economize would come in handy."

Finally, she smiled, and it was like the first sight of sun in February. "Well, then, I'm your gal."

And there it was, his opportunity.

Yes, you are my gal, the only one I'll ever need. Will you do me the honor of marrying me?

It was a good proposal, one that would likely please her, but no words came out of his mouth. Maybe if he eased into it instead, he could get the words out.

"Well, then," he said, every muscle tensing as if she'd pulled a pistol on him, "when we're married, would you prefer to tend the house or work more on the ranch?"

She stared at him, and his heart shriveled. She licked her lips. She was going to refuse!

"When we're married," she said slowly, as if waiting for him to correct her, "will we have a home? Will you claim land? I think that's what you call it in the territories."

She hadn't said no. Air filled his lungs, relief his chest. He nearly slumped in the chair.

"That's the process. But most of the land in the area has been claimed. That's why Mr. Dalrymple needed someone to sell or give him land to build a church. Besides, I don't want to be too far from the family." He swiveled in the chair to face her more fully. She was watching him, brow furrowed, and he couldn't tell if that was a sign that she was considering his words or getting ready to refute them.

"What I've been thinking is maybe a house of our own," he confessed. "Out by the drop."

Her frown eased. "I can't imagine anything finer than waking up each morning with that view."

Unless it was waking up next to her.

CHAPTER THIRTEEN

WHEN WE'RE MARRIED.

Caroline held the words to her heart as she and Jeremy joined his family for dinner. Perhaps it had been a slip of the tongue, but clearly Jeremy was thinking about a future together. And that's what mattered most.

Ned had returned from his jaunt and took his place beside Joanna, though Jane and Jason were missing. They were out watching the cattle, and Mrs. Willets had put aside food for them to eat later.

"Now that the painting is done," Jack said after Mr. Willets had said the blessing and they were passing around the roast, carrots, and potatoes, "we need to prepare the kitchen garden for the spring. I want to start planting as soon as we can after the last frost. Jacob and Jeremy, I could use your help."

Jacob nodded, but their mother pointed a wooden spoon at Jack. "None of that now. I said Jeremy's one job is courting, and I meant it."

Ned chuckled. "Must be nice, having courting be your job." He nudged Joanna, who sent him a look under her lashes.

Caroline waited for Mrs. Willets to comment on the sly glances. Surely she'd noticed the way Ned and Joanna were behaving.

Instead, she focused on Jeremy. "And how is courting going?"

Now she and Jeremy were the center of attention.

"Rather well, if I do say so myself," Jeremy replied with a grin before popping a slice of carrot into his mouth.

His mother waited while he took his time chewing. So did Caroline. This was his chance to declare his intentions in front of his whole family.

"And?" his mother prompted when he finally had to swallow.

Jeremy took Caroline's hand, fingers warm and strong. "A courtship is between the gentleman and the lady. I'm sure you can understand."

Caroline held back a sigh.

His mother shook her head and returned to her dinner. "Fine. Perhaps the two of you can wash the dishes tonight. *That* will give you more time together."

"Nothing like soap suds to further romance," Jeremy joked.

Caroline couldn't help her giggle, but she couldn't leave it at that.

"Your mother isn't going to give up," she warned him as they stood side by side at the porcelain sink, a tub of sudsy water in front of him and a tub of fresh water in front of her. Jenny had popped several loaves of bread into the oven to bake for the morning, and the yeasty smell vied with the fresh scent of soap.

"I've been fending her off all my life," he replied, handing Caroline a plate to rinse and dry. "I've become an expert. But if you're worried, we could escape tomorrow after breakfast."

She peered up at him. "How?"

His shoulder brushed hers. "As soon as the rain stops, we'll go for a ride. We could go to the, er, drop."

He said the word casually, but she understood what he was suggesting.

They could ride to the drop and share another kiss.

She fluttered her lashes and nodded agreement, afraid of what might pop out of her mouth if she spoke.

Maybe tomorrow, Jeremy would propose.

Just the possibility made it hard to sleep that night, and she was unaccountably jittery when Joanna came to help her with her hair the next morning. At least Ned was already downstairs, so she didn't have to contend with her brother.

"He's a hard worker," Joanna said as she braided Caroline's hair into two plaits down her back, "always willing to lend a hand, like you."

"And that's a welcome surprise," Caroline assured her.

Joanna smiled as she tied the ends off with a pink ribbon, then turned to give Caroline access to her fiery hair. "Do mine the same way. And your influence on Jeremy is a welcome surprise too. He always seemed to laugh things off and go his own way before you arrived."

Caroline cocked her head, working on making Joanna's thick curls behave. "He does like to joke. But I see how hard he works."

"Sometimes I think he fends people off because he isn't sure of them," his sister said, shifting on the bed. "He was the littlest boy for a while when Jesse and Jack were young. They didn't always include him, Jane told me. Jane just forced her way into the thick of things. Still does. But Jeremy made jokes, and that usually got their attention."

Hard to think of Jack or any of Jeremy's siblings thinking less of him, but she could see how Jeremy might have had to work to fit in as a child. His mother and father included all their children in the running of the ranch and family games. Perhaps Jeremy had still felt like an outsider.

She knew the feeling.

She tried not to study him as they ate breakfast that

morning, but her jitters returned in full force as Mrs. Willets reminded everyone of their tasks for the day.

A ride to the drop. A look at the glorious view. A proposal of marriage.

Perhaps an even more glorious kiss?

"Ready to go?" Jeremy asked with a smile as they rose from breakfast.

She nodded eagerly.

Mrs. Willets rose as well. "I need Caroline for a bit this morning. I'd like to make sure I have her measurements correct for that riding skirt."

Jeremy's shoulders slumped.

"Of course, Mrs. Willets," Caroline said, resigned to being helpful. His mother was taking the time to sew her a skirt, after all. She followed the lady from the room.

Mr. and Mrs. Willets's bedchamber was at the back of the house, across the corridor from the kitchen. It was papered in tiny pink rosebuds, and the four-poster bed held pride of place in the center. Mrs. Willets positioned Caroline in front of a tall standing mirror.

"What do you think?" she asked, draping a length of navy serge across Caroline's arm. "Will this do for a riding skirt?"

"It's lovely," Caroline assured her. "Thank you!"

Mrs. Willets smiled as she turned to set the material down on the colorful quilt that covered her bed. "It will go nicely with your dark coloring. My girls look better in greens and browns." She took a length of cord knotted at various internals from her apron pocket and wrapped it around Caroline's waist. Caroline lifted her arms to keep them out of the way.

"Commendable," Mrs. Willets said as she counted the knots. She glanced at Caroline's face. "Are your stays comfortable?"

"Yes, ma'am!" Caroline told her. "I don't over-lace."

She'd never gone along with the idea that ladies needed to cinch themselves tight to fit some fashion.

"Very wise," Mrs. Willets agreed. "Hold this at your waist."

Caroline accepted the end of the measuring cord while Jeremy's mother dropped the other end to the floor and bent to count the number of knots. "And are you satisfied with my son's courtship?"

Caroline jerked, and his mother tsked. "Hold still, dear."

She froze, though she couldn't help drawing in a breath along with a prayer for wisdom. Surely no man wanted a bride who ran telling tales to his mother!

"Jeremy is very attentive," she said. "I appreciate his patience in teaching me about riding and such."

"Attention and patience, two qualities I don't generally associate with my third son. What made you decide to answer his ad? That's how these things go, isn't it? A gentleman places an ad for a mail-order bride? Or did you place the advertisement?"

"It was his," Caroline said as his mother straightened. "I decided to apply to be a mail-order bride because I felt out of place in Cincinnati. So many of the girls I'd gone to school with were married and having children. Those that weren't were very focused on finding a husband. And I never ended up meeting a gentleman who touched my heart."

His mother regarded her as she straightened. "And Jeremy's letters, they touched your heart?"

"Very much so," Caroline told her. "He didn't drone on about his own accomplishments like men tend to do when they're trying to impress. He shared stories about his family, and his love for you all shone through. I thought a man who could love like that might be able to love me." She had to drop her gaze. She'd never confessed that to anyone else. And Jeremy had never claimed to love her.

"I'm glad you were the one who answered his ad," Mrs. Willets said softly, her hand coming to touch Caroline's. "Those are the most important things in life, in the end—finding your own family, where you are loved and appreciated. You both deserve that."

She pulled back, and Caroline raised her head in surprise.

Mrs. Willets had returned to her usual bustling. "Now, I've kept you too long. I believe you and Jeremy were intending to go for a ride." She winked at Caroline. "I wouldn't want to keep you from the drop."

Cheeks heating, Caroline thanked her and hurried back to the kitchen.

Jenny was there, making another batch of bread dough. She smiled at Caroline as she stirred the ingredients together, flour speckling one cheek. "Jeremy said to tell you he'll wait for you in the barn." She too winked.

Did everyone know they were going to the drop?

She hurried out to the barn under a sky that grew lower every moment. She didn't see Jeremy, though both Calico and Quicksilver stood saddled in the fenced area, so she strode into the shadows of the big building. It took a moment for her eyes to adjust to the dim light. Then she spotted Ned in one of the stalls.

He was kissing Joanna.

"Ned!" His name broke past her lips before she could think better of it.

Joanna yanked herself out of his arms. One look at Caroline, and her cheeks darkened. She picked up her skirts and dashed out of the barn.

Ned stomped out of the stall to glare at Caroline. "What? At least I'm brave enough to show a woman how I feel." He stalked after Joanna.

Caroline shook her head to clear it. What had the world come to? Her little brother, claiming to have feelings for a woman after knowing her only a few days? Worse, implying Jeremy was a coward?

Jeremy was brave. Look how he went out at night to tend the cattle. Look at how he stood up to his mother! Look how he rode, all confidence and skill.

And yet, he hadn't proposed yet, his offer to visit the drop notwithstanding.

Could he be afraid of her?

Jeremy wasn't sure why Caroline kept glancing at him as they rode away from the barn. By the way she'd blushed and nodded at his suggestion about riding to the drop last night, she must have some idea of his intentions.

He'd answered a question from Jack, who was gathering the spades to start work on the garden, and returned to find Caroline waiting by the paddock, fingers pleating the riding skirt Jenny had loaned her. This time he lifted her into the sidesaddle, relishing the feel of her, then stepped back as she adjusted her skirts.

Today was the day. Today, he'd propose. Today, he'd become an engaged man.

The sky didn't seem to think much of his chances as he and Caroline followed the track leading east. Clouds obscured the horizon in a mass of boiling black. No sight of the mountain. They'd have rain again soon.

They passed the garden where his family grew the crops for the dining table. Jack, Jacob, and Ned were bending their backs to overturn the rich, black earth.

"Your brother's certainly trying to prove himself," Jeremy mused.

"He's certainly trying," Caroline said tartly. "That much we can agree on."

Jeremy chuckled. "Well, Jack won't let him get away with much."

"Too bad Jack can't be everywhere," she muttered.

From behind them came a yell, and he swiveled in the saddle to find Joy waving a dish towel at them. He reined in Quicksilver, and Caroline stopped Calico to glance back as well.

"Were we supposed to help with the washing or something?" she asked him.

Jeremy shook his head. "Not that I know of." Once, he might have been tempted to ignore his little sister's call. After all, he was about to propose! But something in him urged caution. His parents had enough to contend with. Best he help where he could.

But that didn't mean he and Caroline couldn't have a little fun on the way.

He gathered the reins. "Let's see what she wants. You wanted to gallop. Are you ready?"

Her grin made the grim day brighter. Then she bent over Calico's ears. "You can beat him to the barn, can't you, sweet girl? Go!"

She clapped her heels to the paint's side, and Calico trotted obediently forward, picking up speed with each step.

Jeremy shook his head as Quicksilver danced in anticipation. "Let's give them a little head start."

Quicksilver snorted as if much put out.

Jeremy waited until Caroline was halfway to the barn, then dug his heels in. Quicksilver bolted.

He bent low, the cool, moist wind whipping past. They were close, closer, almost there…

And Caroline managed to reach the barn a good length ahead. By the way her eyes lit, he couldn't mind in the slightest.

"I did it!" she crowed. Immediately, she patted Calico on the shoulder. "We did it, I should say."

"You did indeed," Jeremy said, dismounting. "I own myself conquered." He came around and lifted his arms, and Caroline slid down into them. For a moment, he stood, watching the light shine in her eyes, the color blaze across her cheeks. He was bending his head when Joy came running up, and Quicksilver shied.

"Hurry, Jeremy! Mr. Dalrymple is here, and he's asking for Caroline."

Caroline stepped away from him. "Why would your minister want to talk to me?" She glanced at Jeremy as if sure he'd had something to do with it.

He spread his hands. "I have no idea."

When they reached the parlor, Mr. Dalrymple rose from where he had been seated near Ma and came toward Caroline to take both her hands in his, forcing Jeremy to step back.

"Miss Cadhill," he said, eyes shining, "you have my everlasting thanks."

Caroline looked around him to Ma, who had her fingers pressed to her lips. Joy wiggled onto the sofa beside her, smile huge.

"For what?" Caroline asked, refocusing on Mr. Dalrymple.

"For your generous donation," he said. "I imagine you preferred it to remain anonymous, but I had to come thank you personally. Because of you, we can buy that land and build the church!"

CHAPTER FOURTEEN

JEREMY STARED AT her. Surely Caroline hadn't had the money to help the church. She'd looked so sad when she hadn't been able to contribute to the offering on Sunday.

"It wasn't me," she blurted out. "I don't have any money."

Mr. Dalrymple released her, but he kept beaming at her. "Now, there's no need to be humble. It had to be you. I know all the members of my flock and what they offered to give. The money that appeared at my door yesterday afternoon came with a note saying to use it for good. I just wanted you to know that we will."

"But…" Caroline started.

Ma rose. "Let me get you some tea, Mr. Dalrymple."

He held up a hand. "No need. I won't take any more of your time. I need to notify Mr. Henshaw that we'll accept his kind offer. And I can't wait to telegram my wife. With a house already built and furnished on the property, she can come out and join me after Easter."

"It will be a pleasure to welcome Mrs. Dalrymple," Ma said, walking him toward the door. "You must come to dinner as soon as she arrives." She sent Jeremy a pointed look as she passed.

What, did she expect him to wring a confession out of Caroline? He felt as at sea as Caroline looked.

She sank onto the closest chair. "But it wasn't me," she protested.

"And so you told him," Jeremy assured her, taking the chair nearest hers. "If he insists on giving you the credit, that's his issue."

But it quickly became their issue.

They never did reach the drop that day. First, Ma insisted on an explanation. By the time she was convinced it was all a mistake, Pa and the others started coming in, and Caroline had to explain all over again.

"Someone will claim credit on Sunday," Pa predicted. "This is merely a tempest in a teapot."

And just when Jeremy thought he might extract her, the skies opened, and the rain poured down, destroying any chance of a leisurely ride. He would have gladly kissed Caroline in the rain, but somehow he doubted she'd be quite so enamored by the idea.

Jack and Jacob kept patrolling, regardless of the weather. He supposed rustlers might still strike in a storm, but it seemed unlikely. His other brothers and Ned holed up in the barn with the horses. His mother organized a sewing circle to make clothing for Mrs. Larsen's baby. Since Ma wouldn't hear of him leaving Caroline's side, he found himself in the parlor, darning a sock.

"This is good experience for you, Jeremy," Jane said when Ma and Jenny had gone to check on the bread and begin the dinner preparations. "You can do the mending while Caroline is working with the cattle."

"And I thought *I* was the tease," Jeremy quipped.

"I'd like to learn more about the cattle," Caroline said as if speaking to the tiny shirt she was sewing. "Perhaps you'd be willing to teach me, Jane."

"Happy to oblige," Jane said, taking a stitch in a little cap. "It's not hard."

"Stay away from either end," Joanna agreed, untangling some yarn. "You'll be fine."

"Caroline wouldn't have to help with the cows," Joy put in, trying to knot her thread, "if we had a dog."

"We're not getting a dog, Joy," Jane said. "You heard Pa."

"People can change their minds," Joy insisted. "It just takes a while to sit and think. Right, Jeremy?"

Jeremy raised his brows. "I'm not usually the sit and think sort of fellow."

His littlest sister frowned. "Yes, you are. That's why you haven't married Caroline yet. Ma said you had to sit and think."

Caroline regarded him at last, dark eyes as stormy as the day. "Is that what it takes?"

"No," Jeremy said. He gave it up and tossed the sock to Jane, who caught it. "Ma wants Caroline and me to court, Joy. If painting barns, washing dishes, and darning socks isn't courting, I'm apparently doing it wrong. I should help Jack with the cows."

He strode out of the room, feeling as if a pack of Joy's dogs was nipping at his heels.

Caroline heaved a sigh as Jeremy disappeared out the door. Not only had she not received a proposal, but she was starting to fear she never would. At least not from Jeremy. And that thought made her ache all over.

"Maybe he needs to walk and think instead," Joy said, though her round face was puckering.

"He'll come around," Jane predicted, setting aside the sock Jeremy had tossed at her. "He likes you, Caroline. Anyone can see that."

Several young men in Cincinnati had claimed to enjoy her company. They hadn't proposed either. And none of them had made her smile the way Jeremy did. None of them had looked at her with a mixture of admiration and awe like he did. And none of them had made her tingle all over as if Christmas had come early.

"Joy," Joanna said, winding the yarn into a ball, "I left my best needles upstairs on the dressing table. Would you fetch them for me?"

Joy hopped off the sofa. "Happy to oblige." She skipped from the room.

Joanna leaned back and craned her neck as if to make sure she'd gone. Then she looked to Caroline. "I can explain what you saw in the barn."

This was the first they'd had a moment to talk after that kiss Jeremy's sister had shared with Ned.

Jane frowned. "What happened in the barn?"

Joanna kept her gaze on the yarn as the ball slowly grew under her fingers. "I was asking Ned about his travels, and one thing led to another and…" Her hands stilled. "I kissed him."

Caroline dropped the shirt she'd been sewing. "*You* kissed *him*?"

"Oh, Joanna," Jane said.

Joanna's head came up at last, silvery gray eyes flashing. "Don't you scold me, Jane Wilhemina Willets!"

Jane flinched, but not entirely at the use of the middle name, Caroline thought. "I wasn't scolding. I'm just worried for you."

So was Caroline. Ned could be charming when he set his mind to it, but her brother was in no situation to think about taking a bride. And some would have harsh words for a young lady who kissed and didn't marry.

But she could hardly mention the fact when she was in the same position!

"You needn't worry," Joanna said, returning to her work. "It was an aberration. I don't intend to kiss every handsome wanderer who happens upon the ranch."

And what about her brother? He'd had a hand in all this too. Caroline found her voice. "Unless I'm much mistaken, Ned kissed you back. He obviously admires you. After you left, he claimed he was brave enough to show a woman how he felt. If you have any doubts about my brother's intentions, I'd ask him."

Jane nodded, her own work clearly forgotten. "Wise advice. I'm sure you'll do the same with Jeremy, Caroline."

Caroline swallowed as both sisters watched her.

"Perhaps I will," she said.

When she had an opportunity with no audience!

That Sunday was the Abercrombys' turn to host services. Their farm stood to the north of the Jumping J. It only took a quarter hour for the horses to carry the wagon along the muddy road toward Puget City and up the track that led to the sprawling, single-story farmhouse, but Ma liked to arrive early so she could chat. That meant an early rising, a hurried breakfast, and helping with the harness and tack.

At least the rain held off while they bundled the ladies into the wagon bed. They all wore coats over their good dresses, and bonnets on their hair, but Ma insisted on tucking quilts around them as well. Joshua and Jason rode on the bench with Pa, and Jeremy, Jack, and Jacob rode their own horses. After a hushed conversation with Caroline, Ned had also mounted up and rode with them.

Jeremy hadn't been able to find the right time yesterday for a proposal, but he was more hopeful for today as he nudged Quicksilver closer to the wagon. Jason had fashioned that collar from his mink pelt. It sat on Caroline's coat now, the fur brushing her neck. She looked flushed and happy, her face turned up to a stray bit of sunlight spearing through the clouds.

"No sunbeam will ever look as pretty as you, Miss Cadhill," he told her.

She tossed her head. "Like your sister, I recognize the butter boat too, Mr. Willets."

He would have been discouraged if she hadn't fluttered her lashes at the same time to show she was teasing. He grinned.

Pa turned the horses onto the Abercromby drive, only to be met by a pack of barking dogs. Quicksilver didn't so much as pause, but Jacob had to calm his mount.

Joy reached down a hand as if hoping to catch one of the pups.

"Keep all parts on yourself in the wagon, young lady," Ma ordered her, and his littlest sister settled back with a martyred sigh.

They pulled in among the other wagons. Jack set about taking the team to one of the pastures to wait with some of the horses. Jeremy came around to help the ladies down. Jane cast him an arch look before making way for Caroline.

He lifted her to the ground, holding her a moment longer than necessary—they were courting, after all. She peered up at him as if hoping for more.

"Miss Cadhill," Mr. Abercromby said, shouldering his way into their midst. "Good to see you again."

Caroline turned to smile at him. "Good to see you too, Mr. Abercromby. I stayed longer than either of us expected."

Jeremy wasn't sure what she meant, but the farmer was already motioning to someone else, and his son edged forward. He was only a few months older than Joshua, all gangly arms and legs, with pimples vying with freckles to take up the most of his square face.

"This here's my boy, Tom," Mr. Abercromby said, patting his son fondly on the back. "You didn't get a chance to meet him last Sunday, but since young Jeremy here hasn't popped the question yet, I understand, I thought you'd want to get to know him. Say your how-de-dos, Tom."

Tom grimaced, face reddening, as he stuck out his hand. "How do you do, Miss Cadhill?"

"Very well, Mr. Abercromby," she acknowledged. "Thank you."

Before she could ask after Tom, Jeremy took her hand as they disengaged and tucked it into his arm. "We wouldn't want to be late to services. Excuse us."

He deftly led her back into the center of his family.

"Surely he didn't expect his son to court me," Caroline murmured, glancing back at their host, who was following as close as propriety would allow.

"Doesn't matter," Jeremy said. "You're with me, until you tell me otherwise."

She frowned, but he was relieved she didn't protest as he led her into the house and secured them a spot.

The Abercrombys didn't have as many members of the family as the Willetses, or chairs, so they'd had to improvise for seating. They'd set planks across logs to make two rows of pews across the top of the room, with more chairs lined up behind. Mrs. Abercromby had left one chair and a side table at the front for Mr. Dalrymple.

Jeremy put Caroline at the end of one of the rows and sat next to her, preventing anyone else from getting close. Jane, Jacob, and Jenny filled the rest of the pew. Ma, Pa, and some of the others settled behind them. Ned made sure to sit next to Joanna. Jack made sure to sit next to Ned.

Mr. Dalrymple rose to start the service. "Before we begin," he said, "I want to thank the good Lord for His provision. Because of the kindness, nay, I say, excessive generosity, of one of our members, we have enough money to purchase the Henshaw property and build our church!"

Applause broke out, along with a few whistles. Jeremy

tensed, but the minister did not mention their benefactor's name. Instead, Mr. Dalrymple launched into the opening prayer, then began leading a hymn. Jeremy relaxed.

Still, as the service progressed, he spotted more than one gaze directed Caroline's way, and all from gentlemen. He edged a little closer and stretched his arm around her shoulders. She started, but she didn't pull away. In fact, she fit against him so perfectly they might have been made for each other.

"We haven't had a parade since the Centennial celebration last July," Mr. Dalrymple said when it came time for his sermon. "Many of you attended that to-do in Puget City. The children marched waving flags, and Bill Egbert pounded that drum of his for all he was worth."

Several chuckled. Like Jeremy, they must remember the storekeeper's pride and utter lack of rhythm.

"The crowds were no less enthusiastic as they accompanied our Lord into Jerusalem," their minister continued. "They waved palm branches and marched to the chant, *hosanna in the highest*. And they didn't need anyone drumming."

A few folks nodded. Caroline was watching in that avid way she had, as if she was considering each word.

"Now, I think we all agree that we're still friends with old Bill even though many months have passed," Mr. Dalrymple said with a smile that quickly faded. "But that wasn't the case with this crowd. The same people who praised the Lord as He entered the city called for His death only a week later!"

Caroline shivered and dropped her gaze. He understood. At times, he'd said something or done something in jest, only to have his family fail to appreciate his wit. It had felt like a betrayal. How much worse the Lord must have felt, even though He'd predicted just such a calamity.

"Fickle," Mr. Dalrymple said with a shake of his head.

"Fair-weather friends, their affections blowing away at the first hint of a storm."

Caroline fussed with the button on her coat. Jeremy swallowed. Did he seem like a fair-weather friend to her, kissing her one day and then not proposing the next? How could he explain his conflicted feelings without hurting her further?

The local bachelors were more devoted. Even though Jeremy put himself between them and Caroline after services, they crowded to meet her once more. As if in defense, Caroline latched onto Jane as well.

"Tell Ma we're leaving," Jeremy said around Caroline to his sister. "I'll bring the wagon back once I know Caroline is safe."

"Ma won't like it," Jane predicted. "She'll think Caroline's popularity will only make you jealous."

And she wasn't far off. Already he wanted to shout at that one, shove another out of the way.

"Tell her if I don't take Caroline home now, she'll be engaged to someone else by dinner."

Jane grinned. "That ought to do it. Meet you at the wagon."

She barreled through the men, leaving a gap that quickly closed in her wake.

Somehow, Jeremy managed to get Caroline out of the house without punching anyone.

"I thought they understood I was courting you," she protested as he helped her up into the wagon bed. "Why do they persist?"

"Crows," Jane proclaimed, joining them. "Anything new and shiny attracts their attention."

Still, her admirers persisted. Sunday afternoon, Monday, and Tuesday, they showed up from just after dawn until nearly dusk, giving him and Caroline no moment alone. Ma acted as hostess to the many callers, but she soon had to enlist Jane's and Jenny's help as well.

He had to own himself perplexed. Local men, men who could see her in services, he understood. But he hadn't met half of the callers. They came from Puget City to the north, Olympia to the southwest, and Tenino to the south. Some, like Tom Abercromby, were young enough to be her little brother. Others, like Mr. Ballus, were old enough to be her father. Both had renewed their interest, despite Jeremy's presence at her side.

By Wednesday, he and Jane were forced to stand just inside the parlor door, because there wasn't a seat left open. Ma was on the sofa with Jenny. Caroline had chosen one of the chairs, and Tom Abercromby had stationed himself as close as possible, with Mr. Ballus on her other side. A Mr. Turner and a Mr. Pence from Tenino filled the remaining seats, with two more men leaning up against the opposite wall. They wore the sawdust-flecked trousers that proclaimed them millworkers, most likely from Puget City.

Jason bumped past Jane and Jeremy, bringing in two of the chairs from the dining room for the visitors.

"I don't recall the parlor ever being this full," Jeremy murmured to his sister, "unless it was for a church service."

Jane scowled, arms crossed over her chest. "And where have they been before now? I've been old enough to marry for three years, Jenny for one, and Joanna for a few months."

The man nearest them glanced back over his shoulder. "But you're not an heiress. Any lady that can afford to buy a ranch on a whim is a lady I want to meet."

Caroline must have heard him, for she rose. Most knew enough about manners that they popped up as well, though a couple were slow in copying them and looked around as if mystified.

"Gentlemen, I keep trying to explain, but I don't think you're listening. I'm not an heiress. My father isn't dead, and he'll have nothing to leave me when the time comes."

"Because he already gave it to you for your dowry, I heard," Ballus put in. "Mighty generous, just like you."

"With that kind of money, you can do better than a ranch hand," one of the men from Puget City assured her.

Jeremy pushed off from the wall. "Better than a millworker too."

Caroline hurried to his side and clung to his arm, gaze imploring. "I don't think I could do any better than my intended. I have no reason to look for another husband, do I, Mr. Willets?"

CHAPTER FIFTEEN

H E HARDLY WANTED to propose with this kind of audience. His mother had her brows up expectantly as it was, and three of the men were bristling.

Jeremy took her other hand and brought it to his lips to press a kiss against her knuckles instead. "No, ma'am."

All the men sagged, muttering.

Ma stood. "Well, thank you for visiting, gentlemen. I hope we can count on your support when it comes time to raise the roof on the church. Jane, see them out."

Jane dropped her arms. "They know where they came in. They can see themselves out." She turned and disappeared down the hallway.

Ma frowned after her, but Jenny hurried to escort the men. Each one of them cast Caroline a mournful glance as he passed.

"I'm glad none of them moved you," Jeremy said, lowering her hand.

She shuddered. "Not for a moment. If Jane or Jenny want one, they can have him."

"It may be a while before the tide turns," Ma said, coming to join them. "Gossip like this spreads faster than the truth."

Caroline turned to his mother. "And it is the truth,

Mrs. Willets. If I had that kind of money, I wouldn't have shown up at your door begging for a place."

The words smacked into him like a pickaxe on a boulder. Why had he forgotten she'd only come to find him in desperation? Given any other choice, she would have stayed in Cincinnati.

Ma patted her hand. "I have the riding skirt tacked together in my bedroom. Why don't you go try it on and see if it fits properly?"

With a grateful smile, she fled.

Jeremy picked up one of the chairs from the dining room. "I bet you'll be glad when these callers finally decide it's not worth the bother."

"They might not even arrive at the door if you married her," his mother retorted, hands on her hips. "Do you love her?"

He reared back. Was that what was keeping him from proposing? Did some part of him cling to his parents' impossible dream of true love?

And yet, what he was beginning to feel for Caroline didn't seem so very distant from that dream.

He glanced down the hallway. No one was in sight, but he dropped his voice anyway before answering his mother. "Maybe?"

Ma shook her head. "That's not good enough."

"Neither is much of anything I've ever done," Jeremy teased, though her comment dug into him anew, "so I'm not sure why you're surprised."

She dropped her arms and swatted his hand. "You've done many noteworthy things over the years, Jeremy Dalton Willets. I remember the time Jenny fell from her horse, and Doctor Rawlins said we shouldn't allow her to fall asleep. You stayed up with her all night, and you kept her from fretting."

He'd forgotten about that incident. "Well, someone had to do it."

"I don't know any of us who could have done it better," his mother insisted. "And who got Jason and Joshua to sit through their lessons when all they wanted to do was run off into the woods and explore?"

Jeremy wiggled his brows. "Bribery of a horse ride will get you far, dear lady."

She shook her head again. "Only when you know you can trust the person doing the bribing. You have been the heart of this family since the day you were born."

He swallowed, throat suddenly tight. "I never knew you felt that way."

"Then I've been lax in my duties." She leaned over and pressed a kiss to his cheek. "You are and always will be my darling boy. But, knowing you have a big heart, I want to make sure you share it with the right woman. Marriage lasts your entire life, if you're fortunate. You want to wake up every morning and feel blessed by the person beside you. Blessed, and maybe a little humbled that they chose you."

Her words tugged at him. He'd never thought he would find such a love after Deborah, but now, when he looked into Caroline's eyes, he saw the possibility of such a future. If only she saw the same future, with him.

He made himself shrug. "She didn't have much of a choice. She needed help, and I offered."

"Well, she has plenty of choices now," his mother reminded him. "She's a sweet, upstanding young lady, Jeremy, who clearly sees the best in the world. If you don't snap her up, someone else will."

Jeremy blew out a breath as his mother marched down the hall for her room. She was right. Every day he found more things to admire about Caroline. She was willing to work at anything if it helped someone else. And she was willing to try things that scared her. He'd seen the way she'd looked at Calico the first time they'd gone riding. He found he could even tolerate her brother.

But just because his mother could see into his heart didn't mean Caroline could or that she would like what she found.

He focused on returning the chairs to the dining room and setting the parlor to rights. The next time a fellow showed up at the door, he'd send him packing. Caroline deserved better than to be forced on display like a doll in the mercantile window at Christmas.

She met him as he was coming out of the parlor. Her head was cocked, and a frown hovered.

"Skirt not fit?" he asked.

She waved a hand. "It fits perfectly. Your mother is very good with a needle. I'm more concerned about you."

Jeremy smiled at her. "Me? Why? No one's challenged me to a duel in your honor. Yet."

"No one's offered to marry me yet either." She met his gaze. "Please, Jeremy. Tell me the truth. Are you afraid of me?"

He stiffened. "What? No! Why would you think that?"

His brows were up, his shoulders too. Caroline had finally had a moment alone with Jeremy to ask, and she wasn't sure whether to feel relieved that he was shocked she'd suggest such a thing or depressed that his hesitation stemmed from something more.

Something worse.

She couldn't look at him any longer, dropping her gaze to the hem of her gown instead. "Well, I answered your ad for a mail-order bride and journeyed to the Jumping J, and you haven't proposed for all you tell others we're promised. I thought maybe I'd done something, said something…" She wasn't sure how to finish, wasn't sure she wanted to hear him say that she hadn't measured up.

Instead, he took her hand and drew her into the dining

room. No one would be using it for a few hours, so perhaps they'd have some privacy. As if he thought so as well, he took her in his arms. She leaned into the warmth, wishing it might be hers, forever.

"It's not you, sweetheart," he murmured, cheek brushing her hair. "You are everything I hoped for and more. I'm the one lacking. I've been so sure I'd hear *no* that I never gave you the chance to say *yes*."

Caroline had to pull back so she could see his face. His green eyes sagged, as if he was still sure she was going to refuse him. "Why did you think I'd say no? I came all this way to marry you!"

"And now you know you have other choices," he pointed out.

She shook her head. "Not one better than you."

He gathered her close once more. "You have no idea how you honor me. Remember when I told you that Jacob and I brought two ladies to the drop?"

"Foolish girls who decided they didn't like the ranch," she said primly.

"They weren't the only foolish ones," he murmured. "I made the mistake of proposing to my lady. She demanded to leave."

Anger tightened her hands into fists. "Well, she wasn't just foolish, then. She was unkind and high-handed, and she clearly thought much too highly of herself."

The chuckle rumbling out of him cooled her indignation.

"I see you've met her," he teased.

"I have not had the dubious pleasure," Caroline replied, "but if I do, I'll happily give her a piece of my mind. On the other hand, perhaps I should thank her. If she hadn't refused, you might not have written for a mail-order bride."

"And I'm glad I did," he assured her, "because you answered. Mr. Dalrymple mentioned that we sometimes believe stories that aren't true. Maybe I've been looking at things the wrong way. Maybe her refusal really is a blessing."

She fought the urge to burrow closer. "It's certainly a blessing for me. You are kind and considerate, and you light up any room you enter. I never thought I'd ever find a gentleman who admires me like you do."

His hand stroked her hair, and she closed her eyes and gave in to her longings. Her arms slipped about his waist, and her head rested against his chest.

"Every gentleman should admire you, Caroline. You are resilient, resourceful, and reliable. You say *I* light up the room? You fill it with warmth."

Oh, how she wanted to be that person! Perhaps, by coming here and giving life a try, she already was.

Beyond them, a rap sounded on the front door.

She sighed as they broke apart. "Oh, not another one!"

He winked at her. "I'll make sure this one doesn't linger."

He went into the hallway and opened the door, just as Joy came skipping down the corridor. She must have spotted Caroline in the dining room, for she came to slip her hand into Caroline's.

From her vantage point, Caroline could see a man was standing on the porch. He was tall, and the tailored suit that was so out of place on the prairie failed to hide his considerable girth. A fringe of a gray mustache and beard hid his mouth. He pulled off his top hat to reveal a bald head.

"Sorry to intrude," he said with a nod to Jeremy. "I understand that Miss Cadhill is staying here."

"She's taken," Jeremy said. "A shame you came all this way for nothing."

The man widened his stance as if refusing to budge one inch. "But I'm a friend of the family."

Caroline stepped out of the dining room, bringing Joy with her. "Have we met?"

His face broadened into a smile. "Not formally. I'm Frederick Dickerson. I worked at Cincinnati Savings and Trust."

Fear lanced. "Are you bringing me word about Father? Did something happen?"

He shook his head. "No. He's still in jail as far as I know. I'm sorry about what happened. I had to tell the authorities what I'd seen."

This was the man who had been a witness against her father? It was all she could do to keep the smile on her own face when she wanted to order him off the property. Then again, perhaps he'd been mistaken. He seemed so contrite, bleary blue eyes turning down at the corners.

"Why did you come to the Jumping J, then?" she asked.

Joy squeezed her hand as if pleased to hear her use the name.

"I understood you and your brother had come West, so I wanted to pay my respects while I was in the area. I didn't know you had family out this way."

Jeremy offered his hand as well. "Jeremy Willets."

"And I'm Joy," his sister said, dipping a curtsey as the two men shook hands.

"Come in, Mr. Dickerson," Jeremy said, stepping aside. "We can all be more comfortable in the parlor. Joy, fetch Ned."

His mother must have heard their voices, for she came down the hall and joined them in the parlor. Caroline made the introductions.

"Fine ranch you have here, ma'am," Mr. Dickerson said to Jeremy's mother as he perched on a chair. "Herd of cattle, crops. You've done well for yourself."

"We have made a way in the wilderness," Mrs. Willets agreed with a smile. "And what brings you to the far West?"

Before he could answer, Ned walked into the parlor.

"You wanted me, Mrs. Willets?" He met Mr. Dickerson's gaze, then jerked to a stop, blanching.

Mr. Dickerson stood. "I should be going. I'm staying in Puget City. I hope to hear from you soon, Ned. Ma'am." He bowed his head to Mrs. Willets and brushed past Ned for the front door.

Mrs. Willets frowned as the door shut behind him. "What was that all about?"

Caroline rounded on her brother. "You know, Ned."

Her brother visibly swallowed. "He worked with Father at the bank."

"So he said," Jeremy supplied. "But you turned white when you saw him. Why?"

Ned hurried to Caroline and seized her hand. "We have to leave. Now. The men who threatened you in Cincinnati? They work for him. He's the one who forced Father to take the money. Father gave it to me to hide. And Dickerson wants it back."

Caroline swayed, and Jeremy caught her arm to steady her.

"I think you better explain yourself, Ned Cadhill," Ma said, eyes narrow and voice steely. Ned had obviously dropped in her estimation, and she would likely have used his middle name had she known it.

Ned's gaze was wide and panicked, but Caroline roused herself before he could speak. "Your father, Jack, Jane, and Joanna should hear this as well, Jeremy."

"Not Joanna," Ned put in, voice trembling. "Please."

Caroline hesitated and glanced at Jeremy.

He'd seen the way his sister looked at Caroline's brother. "Not Joanna," he agreed for his sister's sake. "Not yet. But I'll fetch the others." He made sure Caroline was safely seated once more before leaving. Every step seemed a sacrifice when he should be at her side.

Jack grumbled at being forced away from his work, and Jane looked openly curious as Jeremy led them and their father back to the house a short time later. Caroline was still sitting on the sofa, fingers worrying in the lap of her gown. Ma was on a chair a short distance away, watching the door. And Ned was pacing fast enough to wear a track in the plank floor.

He stopped as they came in. Jeremy sat next to Caroline, draping an arm about her shoulders. She smiled at him. Her lips trembled.

"So, what's this all about, son?" Pa asked, looking to Jeremy.

Jeremy squeezed her shoulder. "Would you like me to explain?"

Caroline drew in a breath. "No, I'll start. You all know that my father was a clerk in a bank, and that he was convicted of embezzlement and sent to prison. Ned disappeared, and I came here out of desperation."

He could feel what the story was costing her. Every moment, she grew more tense, as if she thought they would throw her out. She looked to her brother.

Ned stood taller. "What Caroline didn't know was that Father was being threatened. Fred Dickerson, who worked with him at the bank, told him that he and his men would harm me and Caroline if Father didn't do what he asked. Father tried telling the bank manager, but the man told him he was making it up and not to blame an upstanding employee for his mistakes. Dickerson supposedly has friends in high places, but I wonder if that's a story too."

"If he could threaten your father, he could certainly lie about his background," Pa agreed.

Ned nodded. "Father certainly believed his threats. He did what he could to amass a large amount of money by the date Dickerson had set, only, in the end, he couldn't bring himself to hand it over."

He turned to Caroline, eyes pleading. "He didn't want to steal, Caroline. Please believe me. He told me where he'd stashed the money, then turned himself in to the police. He'd hoped they'd believe him, but the bank blamed him. They took our home, our savings, everything. And I couldn't give them the money, or it would have been further proof that Father was guilty."

"So, the bank was made whole," Pa interrupted.

Caroline nodded. "At our expense. Oh, Ned. What did you do with the money?"

"What Father would have wanted," he snapped. "I gave some to Miss Wilmont's Academy for scholarships so more girls could learn. I gave some to the mission by the river to help the poor. But someone must have suspected where the money came from and spoken to the bank, because Dickerson found me. He threatened to hurt you unless I gave him all of it. Well, I didn't have all of it anymore, did I? So, I ran."

"And I came here, never knowing I'd bring trouble to your door." Caroline looked around, then focused on Jeremy, her face pinched and pale. "I am so, so sorry. Ned and I will leave. Perhaps if we give Mr. Dickerson whatever's left, he'll go away."

Ned grimaced. "Nothing left, sis. I gave the rest of it to your minister to build the church."

"That's where the money came from," Ma said with a shake of her head. "I'm not sure we should let Mr. Dalrymple keep it. It's stolen funds."

"Mr. Dalrymple has already paid for the house and land," Pa said. "And the bank received back the money Caroline's father took. As far as I can see, the money used to pay for the church land came from the sale of Caroline's family home and belongings."

"You're very kind," Caroline said, and all of her was

trembling now. "You've all been so kind. We should leave before something worse happens."

Ma and Pa exchanged glances. Jack had his arms crossed over his chest. Jane's face was puckered.

Jeremy rose. "No. I say Caroline stays."

She made a squeak of a protest, but he knew what was right. He also knew what he wanted. He nearly laughed at the realization. He'd been so focused on avoiding the pain of his previous proposal that he'd been blinded to one simple fact.

Caroline accepted him just as he was, and that made him want to be the best for her. Theirs may not have been love at first sight, but he didn't question that love had grown. It pulsed through him now, strengthening his resolve.

A future without Caroline at his side was unthinkable.

Which meant there was only one thing left to do. He went down on one knee in front of her and took her cold hands in his. Those big brown eyes held his just as she held his heart.

"I wrote away for a mail-order bride because I was convinced I'd never find the kind of love my parents had," he told her. "I was wrong. I love you, Caroline Cadhill. Will you do me the honor of marrying me?"

CHAPTER SIXTEEN

O H, THE DEAR man! She'd wondered whether she would ever be a bride, doubted that Jeremy had cared enough to marry her. But he positively glowed with purpose and surety. She felt the same surety rising up inside. She pressed her fingers to her lips in amazement, but the word burst out anyway. "Yes!"

Jeremy rose, and so did she, and in his arms, she knew herself accepted, cherished, loved.

"I love you too," she murmured, drawing back to peer into his face, which looked absolutely besotted. "I think I fell in love a little more with every letter, and I tipped all the way when I finally met you."

"And that is simply perfect!" his mother declared, rising as well. Beaming, she opened her arms and hugged them both.

Caroline closed her eyes and whispered a prayer of thanks, for Jeremy, for his mother, for his whole family. *You accepted me, Lord, just as I am, and so do they. That is a blessing!*

"It may not have happened at first sight," his mother said, drawing back with a watery smile, "but you've each found someone who loves you and will stick by you no matter what. And so will we."

His father came to clap Jeremy on the back, Jane came

to hug her, and Jack shook hands all around. She glanced to where her brother stood, shifting from foot to foot as if afraid he'd have to light out.

Caroline motioned to him with her hand. "Well? Come on!"

With a relieved grin, he came to hug her and shake Jeremy's hand too.

"Now," his father said, face turning stern, "we have some planning to do. We will not be letting this Dickerson fellow win."

"No, sir," Ned agreed, and the others nodded.

"We'll send someone to Puget City to telegraph Sheriff Billings in Olympia," Jack said. "Jason is the fastest rider, and Dickerson may not think him a target since he's younger. The rest of us can circle the herd like we do on cattle drives, watching the edges of the ranch. Nobody gets in or out of the Jumping J without us approving."

"I don't know how many others he has with him," Ned warned. "I saw two the last time he approached me."

"He still has two," Jack said, with a look to Jeremy. "We found evidence of one in the woods the first time. Maybe he followed Caroline from Cincinnati. Either way, they must have realized she was coming to the area, but I doubt they knew which ranch. They likely split up to find her. The first man who spotted her alerted the others, because the next camp we found showed three had been using it."

Caroline swallowed. "Three could cause some trouble."

"Three we can handle," Mr. Willets promised.

Mrs. Willets must have made up her mind, for she nodded. "Jack, you see to Jason and the patrolling. I'd like Jeremy to stay in the house with Caroline."

"I'll take his place," Jane offered. "I can shoot as straight."

"And ride better," Jeremy added with a grin. "Thanks, Jane."

"I can take a shift too," Ned said.

Jack shook his head. "Best Dickerson doesn't have a chance at you."

Ned's face fell.

"Don't worry, Ned," Jeremy's mother said. "I'll find work for you. Easter is only a few days away. We have much to do to prepare."

Bless the dear woman, but she kept them busy the rest of the afternoon. With everything that had happened, Caroline had nearly forgotten that that Sunday would be Easter. Jason had brought home a plump goose, which had to be plucked and cleaned. Jenny was planning a special kind of stuffing that needed herbs to be ground and sifted together. Jeremy's mother wanted the whole house sparkling, which meant window washing, sweeping, and rug beating.

"And then there's what we'll wear," Joanna confided to Caroline as they stood just off the porch before dinner, smacking a rug with latticed wooden beaters. The rain had stopped, but the clouds still hung low, dark and threatening. Jeremy kept watch at the edge of the porch. His gaze drifted to the forest beyond the fields as if he thought Mr. Dickerson was waiting.

Caroline wrinkled her nose as dust puffed out from the rug. "I have three dresses. I'll just wear the nicest."

"I'm sure Jenny would let you borrow something of hers," Jeremy's sister pointed out.

"And everyone would know it was hers," Caroline reminded her.

"Well, you can borrow some of my hair ribbons," Joanna insisted. "They'll look different in your black hair than they would in my red curls in any event." She peered around the rug at her. "Which of my dresses do you think Ned would like best?"

Caroline gave the rug a good smack, sending it swinging toward Joanna. "Any of them. It's not the dress but the lady inside it that my brother likes. Have you spoken with him?"

Joanna smacked the rug back toward Caroline. "Yes. And we are in agreement that we should not refine on a certain matter. We are friends."

She peered around the rug and winked at Caroline. "For now."

Jeremy straightened. "Dinner should be about ready."

Joanna pulled the rug off the line and followed Caroline inside.

She still couldn't quite believe that Jeremy had proposed. He held out her dining chair as if she were a great lady.

"Practicing," he said before dropping into his chair beside her. "I expect to do that every day for the rest of my life and count myself fortunate each time."

"And what if I want to pull out my own chair?" she asked, putting her napkin on her lap.

"Why, I'll look for other ways to serve you," he promised. "I never want you to doubt that you're loved and appreciated."

By the way he looked at her, she had no doubts.

Some of the other members of his family and Ned trickled in to take their places. Jacob leaned over next to Caroline.

"I apologize," he murmured, eyes contrite behind his spectacles. "You obviously have my brother's best interests at heart." His gaze went beyond her to Jeremy. "And I see he learned his lesson well."

Jeremy took Caroline's hand and brought it to his lips for a kiss. "And profited by it, brother."

With a pleased nod, he headed for his own chair.

"Did Jacob have words with you earlier?" Jeremy asked, watching his brother but keeping a hold of Caroline's hand as if to protect her.

"He was protecting you," Caroline assured him. "I didn't know the story about the woman who refused you then, but I think I understand his concerns now. And I know I'll never be so foolish."

"And I am eternally grateful," he told her with a smile.

Finally, the others came in. Jack, Jane, and Joshua were on duty outside, so the table didn't look nearly as full as usual.

And Jason's spot was empty.

Jeremy frowned as his father said the blessing.

"Jason not back yet?" he asked as soon as Mr. Willets finished and the others began passing the food.

"Something's wrong," Mrs. Willets said, clutching the bowl of carrots as if she'd never let go.

Caroline looked to Jeremy's father at the opposite end of the table. His face was grim. "We'll go looking as soon as Jack comes in."

Caroline reached under the table and gripped Jeremy's hand, hard.

"It will be all right," he murmured.

She wished she could believe that. She would never forgive herself if something happened to one of his family because of her.

A door banged, and boots sounded down the hallway a moment before Joshua burst into the dining room. His face was flushed, and his cowlick stood at attention like a red flag.

"Dickerson's out near the forest. He caught Jason before he could reach Puget City. He says if we don't give him his money, he's going to shoot him."

Chairs screeched on wood as they all stood.

"No one's shooting anyone," their father said, striding around the table to put a hand on his son's shoulder, "unless it's that skunk who calls himself a man. Jenny, fetch my rifle. Jane, you still got your pistols on?"

She patted the brace at her hips. "I'm ready, Pa."

No, no, no! This wasn't right! Caroline had been forced to stand by while her father was taken away, tried, and convicted. She'd been forced to wait for Ned alone. She'd waited for Jeremy to decide whether they'd suit.

She wasn't going to sit by this time. She was going to fight for Jeremy and the family she had come to love.

"It's the money he wants," she said, and they all looked to her as if surprised to hear her speak. She could have told them she was a little surprised too. "We should give it to him."

"But I told you," Ned protested. "I don't have it."

"He doesn't know that," Caroline reasoned. "If I stuff my valise and carry it out to him, he'll expect it to be full of money."

"But if he looks," Mrs. Willets started.

"We won't give him time to look," Caroline said. "Jeremy, if I keep him busy talking, can you and the others surround him and his men?"

"Better," he said, jaw hard. "We'll drive the cattle right over them. But I don't like you being in danger, Caroline. Let me carry the bag."

"No," Ned said, moving to her side. "This is my fault. I should be the one in his sights."

"Thank you," Caroline said, catching a glimpse of the loving boy she'd raised. "But you've already lied to him once. He won't trust you. He might trust me. And that's all we need."

Mrs. Willets lifted her chin. "You heard Caroline. She has a plan, and it's a good one. Ned, Joanna, and Jenny go help her stuff that valise and get herself ready. Use whatever you need from our room. Joshua, when we're ready, show her where Mr. Dickerson and his men are. Joe, you walk her part of the way. Jeremy, go tell Jack and the others what you have in mind. Take Jane with you."

"What can I do, Ma?" Joy begged.

Her mother put her arm about her shoulders. "You and I have the most important job of all, honey. We're going to pray."

A short while and an eternity later, Jeremy sat on Quicksilver to the west of the herd. The sky had cleared, leaving behind thin clouds that swept across a nearly full moon and air that was cold and crisp.

Dickerson hadn't brought a lantern. Jeremy could barely make out a smudge against the trees that was the thief, his two men, and Jason. Jack and Jacob had ranged fairly far back into the woods without finding anyone else before coming to join Jeremy.

Caroline, however, was carrying a lantern. It bobbed as she crossed the field, the light turning her gray coat silver and gilding her dark hair. She kept to the far side of the fence that ran from the yard to the woods to prevent the stock from grazing in the kitchen garden. He'd helped repair that fence just last fall. It was a good piece of work.

Now it looked woefully small and worn to protect her from a stampede. What if it didn't hold? What if the cattle pushed through it instead of going through the gate, which Jane crouched waiting to open?

What if Dickerson or his men shot Caroline and Jason as they tried to escape?

No! He couldn't think that way, or he wouldn't be thinking at all. The stakes for being right had never been higher. He couldn't fail her.

"Almost there," Jack said as if Jeremy hadn't noticed. His brother's horse shifted.

"What, nervous?" Jeremy teased. "That's not like you, Jack."

Jack snorted. "I'm not nervous, but I don't see how you can sit there so calmly. That's the woman you claim to love, approaching armed, dangerous men. I'd be going mad."

"Good thing I'm not you," Jeremy said. "All I can think about is protecting her."

"And here I thought I was the wise one," Jacob said approvingly.

Caroline's sweet voice carried across the field. "I have your money." She set down the lantern at her feet, illuminating her slender form. "Let Jason go."

"Toss me the valise, and you can have him," Dickerson said.

"Sorry," Caroline replied, and Jeremy could imagine her wrinkling her nose the way she did. "It's far too heavy for me to toss. What if I set it down between us, and you let Jason join me in the middle? You'll have us both in your sights."

"Seems you're smarter than your brother," Dickerson sneered, "or your father." He must have given Jason a shove, for Jeremy's brother stumbled forward into the light.

Caroline moved closer. Too close. Jeremy gripped the reins, and Quicksilver shied. By the time he had the horse back under control, Jason and Caroline stood together, a few feet away from the scoundrels. Behind them, another shadow rose—Jane, opening the gate.

Dickerson came into the light, his men at his back. He holstered his gun and bent to work at opening the valise.

"Now!" Jeremy cried. They spurred their horses, shouting, and the cattle jerked into motion. The Red Rubies ran, bumping each other, hooves thundering across the field. Jack rode to the north, cutting off their retreat on that side, and Jacob took the south. Jeremy urged Quicksilver right down the middle, hollering at the top of his lungs. Dickerson's men scurried for the protection of the trees.

Dickerson himself was slower to respond. His head snapped up, and the valise fell open, skirts and socks scattering on the grass.

Caroline grabbed Jason's hand, and the two pelted farther back along the fence.

Dickerson reached for his gun.

And then the cattle surged through the gate and thundered toward him. He gave it up and ran for the trees, but he was quickly engulfed and buffeted on every side.

"Jacob and I will take Dickerson and his gang!" Jack shouted to Jeremy. "See to Caroline and Jason."

Jeremy didn't stop to argue. He spurred Quicksilver across the field and through the gate. Vaulting out of the saddle, he ran to Caroline and caught her in his arms, holding her close.

"It's all right," she told him, as if he were the one who needed comforting. "I'm fine, and so is Jason."

"I'm glad to hear it," he said, whispering a prayer of thanks. "But I am never letting you go again."

She giggled, a sound that pushed the darkness away. "That might make it hard to cook or dress, but you won't find me complaining."

Across the field came more shouts. Keeping an arm around Caroline's shoulders, Jeremy turned with her to watch as Joshua and Ned rode out from the barn to begin to calm and collect the cattle. Jane went to mount up as well. Jack and Jacob rode into the light more slowly, prodding Dickerson and his men in front of them. The other two were scruffy fellows, beards untrimmed and clothes worn and patched. Either the bank clerk had turned to two who were down on their luck and desperate enough to help him, or he'd driven them hard enough across the country to bring them to this pass.

"Dickerson has a story to tell the sheriff," Jack said. "As soon as the cows are settled, Jacob and I will take him down to Puget City and telegraph Olympia."

Dickerson's hat was gone, his coat ripped in several places. His men kept eyeing the cattle as if expecting the critters to turn and trample them. If they'd lived all their lives in the city, they probably had no idea how to deal with livestock. Small wonder they'd set up their camps so poorly.

"I need a doctor," one of them complained, cradling an arm.

"I'm sure Sheriff Billings can locate one," Jeremy said. "Though you may have to wait until morning for him to come out from the capitol."

The two men slumped. So did Dickerson. Jeremy didn't feel the least bit sorry for him.

Neither did Caroline, it seemed, for she was more concerned about safety. "Shouldn't we bind them first before transporting them?" she asked his brother.

"I'm not letting anyone in my family close enough to them to try," Jack said. "We'll put them in the wagon, and Jacob can ride with the shotgun. I think I'd take my chances with the sheriff sooner than Sure-Shot Willets."

If Jacob was surprised by the sudden nickname, he didn't show it. Indeed, he scowled so fiercely at the men through his spectacles that they bunched together as if for protection.

Suddenly, Dickerson veered toward Caroline. Jeremy released her, put himself in front of her, and drew his pistol.

Dickerson stopped moving, but he tilted to one side as if trying to see Caroline behind Jeremy. "I could take the blame, Miss Caroline, so your father goes free. All you have to do is put in a good word for me to the sheriff."

The other two started to protest.

"You tell the truth, Mr. Dickerson," Caroline said, voice ringing. "That's the best way to show the sheriff you're remorseful for what you've done."

"Traitor," one of the men muttered as Jack prodded him back with them. "You brought us all this way for a big payout. Now we could hang."

The other man spit on Dickerson's boots.

Jack and Jacob led them all off.

Ned rode up in their stead. Slipping from the saddle, he came to grab Caroline. Jeremy stepped back as her brother twirled her around. "We did it, sis! We're free!"

She righted herself as he set her down. "Jeremy's family did it, Ned. They're the ones you should be thanking."

He stuck out his hand to Jeremy. "Thank you, brother." He grinned. "Funny. I never had a brother before. Now I have five of them!"

"Then I guess I don't have to worry about you and Joanna," Jeremy couldn't help teasing. "After all, she's your sister now."

He almost laughed at the shock on Ned's face.

"When are you going to explain to him that it doesn't work that way?" Caroline asked as Jeremy led her back toward the house. She didn't need his support, but he couldn't have let go of her again if he'd tried. "You'll be his brother-in-law, but the rest of your family isn't actually related to him."

"He seems like a smart lad," Jeremy said. "He'll figure it out on his own. After all, it only took me about three weeks to figure out I wanted to marry my mail-order bride."

CHAPTER SEVENTEEN

CAROLINE HAD COME to the Jumping J all of a sudden, but she was finally going to be a bride. She marveled at the fact over the next few days as they celebrated Easter with Jeremy's family. They might not wait for the wildflowers, or the new church, to marry, but they made other plans for their future.

At least she no longer had to worry about her father. Two deputy sheriffs had taken Dickerson and his men into custody, and the sheriff himself had telegraphed Cincinnati so her father's lawyer could start an appeal, claiming duress. If the judge agreed to be lenient, her father likely wouldn't arrive in time for the wedding, but he might be out of prison by summer!

To her surprise, Ned decided not to stay for the wedding either. He announced his intentions of riding home to make sure their father was released and promised to send the things Caroline had left behind from the lodging house out to her. The entire Willets family turned out to see him off two days after Easter. He shook everyone's hand in turn, saving Joanna for last.

Jeremy's sister shifted on her feet, her gingham skirts swaying, but she kept her chin up. Still, her eyes swam with tears.

Ned offered her his best smile. "I'll come back, Joanna. I promise. It just might take a bit. Will you wait for me?"

Jack sucked in a breath, and Jacob fisted his hands.

Joanna nodded. "I'll wait, Ned. Write to me."

"Yes, ma'am," he assured her. "You can be *my* mail-order bride."

Jeremy's mother didn't look too pleased at the suggestion, but she merely waved with the others as Ned set off down the drive.

As Mr. and Mrs. Willets turned for the house and most of Jeremy's siblings hurried off to their tasks, Jack stepped in beside Jeremy and Caroline.

"I've been thinking," he began, gaze on the distant horizon.

"That usually means trouble," Jeremy said with a wink to Caroline as he slipped his arm about her waist. Oh, but she hoped she would always feel this fierce joy at his touch.

Jack rolled his eyes. "What I was going to say is that Ma and Pa fitted up the old tack room as a bedroom and parlor for me. I think you two should have them after you're married."

Jeremy cuffed him on the shoulder with his free hand. "Thanks, Jack. A very generous offer."

"But we have other plans," Caroline finished. "Jeremy told me about your concerns for your father's health."

Jack's glower descended. She knew now it was more bluster than bite. "We both want to help," she told him. "So, to that end, we have a proposal." She looked to Jeremy.

"We need a bunkhouse," Jeremy told his brother. "We can move Jacob, Jason, and Joshua into it, give them more space than they have in the house. And we'd have space to put up other workers if we needed to ease the load on the rest of us."

Jack nodded thoughtfully. "That might work. So would you and Caroline stay in the house, then?"

"To help Ma and Pa, yes," Jeremy agreed.

Caroline glanced at the big ranch house that had come to mean so much to her. "I love being near your family."

Jeremy tucked her closer. "Our family now, sweetheart." He bent his head and caressed her mouth with a kiss.

Her husband, her love, her future.

And they lived happily ever after, the end, as Joy liked to say.

THANK YOU FOR reading Jeremy and Caroline's story. The Willets family made their debut in *The Schoolmarm's Convenient Marriage*, which tells the story of their brother Jesse's courtship. I had to give the other brothers and sisters a happily-ever-after too.

Want to make sure you have the opportunity to read the rest of their stories? Sign up for my newsletter at https://subscribe.reginascott.com, and you'll receive exclusive free reads, sneak peeks, and news of releases and sales.

After Jeremy's experience with Caroline, you might be wondering whether more mail-order brides might be in the family's future. Turn the page for a sneak peek of Jack's story, *Leftover Mail-Order Bride*.

SNEAK PEEK

Leftover Mail-Order Bride
Book 2 in the Frontier Brides Series
by Regina Scott

Near Olympia, Washington Territory
Late April 1877

DID A MAIL-ORDER bride necessarily require a groom?

The thought pushed Victoria Milford's fingers up and down the keys of the battered upright piano as she tried to focus on the Mozart sonata. Concentrating on the shakes and runs normally chased away any fretting, but today her problems crowded closer than the walls of the little frontier parlor.

Why hadn't he waited? It had only taken fourteen days to travel to Washington Territory from Albany. She had it on good authority there were few eligible ladies along Puget Sound. Had he snatched at any opportunity to avoid marrying her, despite the promise in his letters?

If that was the sum total of a gentleman's faithfulness, maybe having a husband wasn't worth the bother. She'd nursed for most of her life, first her father, then her mother, then cousin Phyllis. The territorial capital and surrounding areas might not have a hospital yet, but surely some physician would appreciate a second pair of hands.

The doctor in Puget City hadn't.

"Sorry, Miss Milford," Doctor Rawlins had said, rubbing his stubbled jaw with the back of one hand. "Much as I could use the help, I can't see bringing on an unmarried lady. It wouldn't be right. But never you fear. A young lady as pretty and talented as you will have no trouble finding another groom."

No, just one she wanted.

She closed her eyes, let her fingers fly up and down the keys, and breathed in the rousing music. *Show me Your will, Father. You must have had a reason for bringing me here.*

Beyond the pounding music, beyond her tumultuous thoughts, another noise intruded. She opened her eyes, expecting to see that her hostess had joined her. Instead, a man was standing in the parlor doorway, watching her, awe stamped on his handsome face. He stood tall and stocky in his rawhide coat and dusty trousers, a dime novel frontiersman come to life.

She might not recognize him, but she recognized admiration when she saw it. The look was balm to her soul after being rejected practically at the altar. Her fingers slowed, stilled.

"Don't stop playing on my account," he said in a warm voice, removing his hat to reveal short-cut hair as fiery red as the feathers of a scarlet tanager. "It would be a shame to keep such beauty from the world."

Her mouth was turning up in a smile before she thought better of it. She pulled back her hands and folded them in the lap of her mint-colored silk gown. "Nonsense. You must have a reason for coming to call. I wouldn't want to interfere."

He opened his mouth as if to explain, but Mrs. Dalrymple bustled in. The minister's wife was short, round, and quick in both action and speech, reminding Victoria of a house wren. Like her, she wore the fine gowns expected of a parlor back East, not the more practical ginghams and calicos Victoria had seen when she'd come West. Her brown curls bobbed beside her face as she glanced between Victoria and the stranger.

"Oh, you've met," she said, rosebud mouth turning down. She sounded almost disappointed.

Why? Was this fellow someone she should avoid? Mrs. Dalrymple had certainly pointed out enough of those since Victoria had arrived three days ago. The clerk at the Egbert mercantile in Puget City with the nice smile had once given incorrect change and was not to be trusted with anything so important as a woman's heart. The rancher who'd offered them a cut of beef whipped his horse and would likely treat his wife and children as badly. The farmer who brought the milk did not tithe to the church, and who wanted a tight-fisted husband?

Besides, Mrs. Dalrymple had confided, every bachelor in the area would think twice before courting someone's leftover mail-order bride. Victoria must study them carefully to know their intentions.

After all, she had little choice. She must either marry or find a position. She certainly couldn't live in the Dalrymples' spare bedroom for the rest of her life. The minister's wife had already erected a sign in the front yard saying *Room for Rent* as if she expected Victoria's tenure to be brief indeed.

"Miss Milford," Mrs. Dalrymple said now, pug nose up in the air as if she'd smelled day-old cabbage, "allow me to introduce Mr. Jack Willets. He's the second son of a local rancher."

Second son generally meant no inheritance was involved, but not always. With those broad shoulders and long limbs, Mr. Willets could likely work at anything he wanted.

"Mr. Willets," she said, inclining her head.

"Miss Milford," he said with a nod that sent light rippling like flame through his hair. "I don't suppose you'd care to take a walk?" He glanced at Mrs. Dalrymple as if seeking her permission as well.

One look, and he wanted to walk out with her? Was he so impetuous, then? Would his interest cool as quickly as Charles' had?

The minister's wife heaved a martyred sigh that raised the ruffles on her generous bosom. "I suppose that would be suitable." She held up one finger. "Just to the end of the drive and back, mind you. Miss Milford has many obligations."

Miss Milford had had many obligations most of her life, from learning to be a lady and all the accomplishments that entailed to caring for her ailing family. At the moment, Miss Milford was blithefully free of obligations.

She rose from behind the piano. "I'll get my coat."

Mr. Willets stepped aside to let her pass, and she caught sight of his eyes. They were the smoky gray to match the fire of his hair. And they were gazing at her as if she were the most amazing person he had ever met. A woman could grow fond of such looks.

Something snagged her skirts, and she glanced back to find that Mrs. Dalrymple had followed her out of the parlor so closely she'd trod on Victoria's hem. The minister's wife tsked as she stepped aside.

"I'll watch from the porch," she murmured with a glance back at the waiting Mr. Willets.

"Is he not to be trusted then?" Victoria murmured back, spirits dipping as she shook out the ruffles along her hem.

"He seems a very responsible gentleman," Mrs. Dalrymple assured her, going to pull Victoria's embroidered wool coat down from the hook by the door. "His parents dote on him. He tithes, and he's been leading the effort to erect our first church building. He does seem a bit bossy. He is in the market for a bride, but when I suggested he might write away for one, he refused." She shook her head as she helped Victoria into her coat. "'Pride goeth before destruction and a haughty spirit before a fall,' you know."

Humility. One more item to add to the list of characteristics Mrs. Dalrymple expected Victoria's husband to possess, along with patience, faithfulness, fiscal responsibility, kindness to animals, and frequent tithing. He would have to be an absolute paragon among men.

She'd never find a groom to match.

Jack slid his hat back on his head, only to pull it off again out of respect as the minister's wife sidled up to him.

"Walk if you like, but she's not a suitable bride for you," she murmured, gaze on Miss Milford's back.

Jack frowned, but Mrs. Dalrymple put on a smile and flapped her fingers, shooing him out of the house as if he were a recalcitrant chicken. Bemused, he followed Miss Milford down the front steps and onto the muddy track that ran out to the country road to Puget City. He'd never accustomed himself to the house that was now being used as the parsonage. Everyone had shaken their heads when the former owner, Mr. Henshaw, had built the four-story narrow monstrosity and painted it a jaunty pink. With all the bric-a-brac edging the roof and windows, it might have graced the richest neighborhood in refined Port Townsend to the north, with other houses close on either side. It looked completely out of place standing alone on the edge of a plateau overlooking Puget Sound, surrounded by nothing but fields and forests.

But it fit the beauty walking beside him perfectly.

She was as unexpected as the house. That dusky red hair was smoothed back in a proper bun, but the arrangement couldn't hide the luster. How Ma would laugh if he brought home another red-head. Their family was filled with them.

And wouldn't Ma be pleased if she knew that he'd taken one look at the lady and toppled like a fir under his brother Jesse's two-handed ax?

Love at first sight? His parents claimed they'd married because of it. He'd thought it a fine story, something endearing to share with their children.

Until Victoria Milford had played that music, and all he could do was stand and stare.

He grimaced now and hoped she hadn't noticed. Love at first sight might be something his parents and the poets celebrated, but he wasn't looking for love. He wasn't looking for a bride only suited to the parlor either. He needed a wife who could be a helpmate, working beside him to care for his family. And if he'd wanted any old bride, he could have written away for a mail-order bride, like his younger brother Jeremy had.

Mrs. Dalrymple must know something about this woman that she hadn't been able to share with Jack to caution him against her. After all, Jack had asked her to help him find a lady to court. The minister's wife was sitting on the porch bench, knitting needles in her hands but gaze watchful. Perhaps she expected him to discover the flaw in this rose.

"Are the Dalrymples your family, then?" he asked.

She picked up her skirts with one hand. Like the rest of her, they were dainty and elegant. His sisters Jenny and Joanna would have swooned at the number of rows of frilly ruffles that covered the bottom third of the dress. Jane would probably have laughed. She understood the need to be sensible.

"No," Miss Mitford said. "They were kind enough to take me in after… I came West."

Single ladies didn't usually travel to the frontier alone, at least not ladies his mother would accept in her house.

"What brought you out this way?" he asked, frowning.

She turned to look at him and jerked to a stop, forcing him up as well. "What is that!"

Had she spotted a bear? A cougar? Jack whirled, hand to the pistol on his hip, but the fields rippled green into the distance, where the mountain rose in all her glory.

He smiled at his companion. "That's Mount Rainier. Is this the first you've seen her?"

She nodded, gaze on the mass of white and silvery rock rising beyond the Nisqually Delta.

"She likes to hide when it's rainy or there's any hint of a cloud between us and her," Jack explained, "but you have to admit she looks rather fine reigning over the area."

"She's beautiful," she said, voice awed.

Yes, Miss Milford was. Her eyes were as brown as a walnut, with flecks of gold as if hinting of something fine, something precious inside. Her lips reminded him of the inside of the shells his sisters like to gather from the shore, though they looked a lot softer and warmer. If he bent closer…

He reined in his thoughts with more difficulty than a runaway horse. He'd just met this woman! Jack swallowed and forced his feet to move again. He was just thankful she fell in beside him.

Still, he struggled to think of what to say next. Too soon to tell her his hopes for a match. Too intrusive to ask if she was itching to wed.

The area. That was a safe topic of conversation. He nodded to the northwest. "The forest is blocking the view, but if you get beyond it, you can see the Olympics across Puget Sound as well. Then there's Mount Saint Helens to the south and Mount Baker to the north. On a clear day, you can see all of them."

"You're ringed by grandeur," she said, shaking her head as if she could hardly believe such riches. "How do you get anything done without standing and shouting a hallelujah?"

He chuckled. "Well, you get used to it after a while."

"I hope I never do," she vowed.

So did he. It would be a shame to lose that light in her eyes.

Apparently, she had questions for him as well, for she cleared her throat and started asking. "Mrs. Dalrymple said you have a ranch nearby, I believe?"

"The Jumping J to the south of us." As soon as he said it, he felt foolish. "My littlest sister named it that. It's a busy ranch, and all our names start with the letter J."

"All?" she asked innocently.

Mrs. Dalrymple must not have mentioned that to her. Not everyone appreciated the size of his family. He'd heard the jokes for years.

Your pa sure must like pups 'cause he has a pack of them.

Why'd he stop at ten? Jesus had twelve apostles.

But any woman who married him had to marry into his family. Supporting them was non-negotiable.

"I'm one of ten," he told her. "My oldest brother, Jesse, lives up at Wallin Landing, near Seattle. Then there's me, Jeremy, Jacob, Jane, Jenny, Joanna, Jason, Joshua, and Joy."

"Joy, who named the ranch," she surmised.

She was quick. Not many would have followed that litany, particularly as he hadn't taken his time spitting it out. "That's right. She's the youngest at ten. Jesse is the oldest at one and thirty."

"What a time your mother must have had," she said, voice sounding awed again. "Ten live births is quite an accomplishment. She must have had a good midwife."

Funny. No one had ever talked about his mother's laying-ins before. Then again, most of the men in the area wouldn't have thought to question how hard it was to birth babies.

"Not many midwives in the area," Jack allowed. Not

many wives of any kind, but if she hadn't figured that out, she would as soon as the other suitors started stampeding to her door.

She made a noise as if deploring the lack of medical care.

"Of course, we have a fine physician," he hurried to add. No sense scaring her off. "Doctor Rawlins comes out whenever we send for him."

"Yes, I've met the good doctor," she said. She didn't sound particularly impressed.

In fact, aside from the view, she didn't seem impressed by much of anything in the area. Who could blame her? Not many were suited to live on the frontier. That's why so few traveled West.

Those who stayed in their big cities back East didn't know what they were missing. Freedom, purpose, a chance to make your own way.

The quiet to worship a God who had created all this for His children.

"You planning on staying in the area?" Jack asked.

She sighed. "Yes, I suppose so. There's nothing for me back home in Albany."

Albany. That was in New York state, if he remembered Ma's geography lessons right. Like Olympia to the southwest, it was the capital. Miss Milford might be used to dealing with governors and legislators, folks who lived in fancy houses and did important things.

Things more important than running a cattle ranch on Hawks Prairie.

The words popped out before he could stop them. "Are you fixing to marry, then?"

She flinched as if the question had taken a bite out of her.

"Sorry for the plain speaking," he tried. "That's my way. Best you know that now."

"I appreciate your candor, Mr. Willets," she said. "Allow

me to offer the same. I am considering marriage as one of my options for my future, and Mrs. Dalrymple has encouraged me to look for a suitable groom, one who meets her criteria for a match."

Mrs. Dalrymple had criteria for husbands? He'd thought the minister's wife hesitant because of Miss Mitford's qualifications, not his.

"Maybe I should talk with the lady," he said, glancing back at the porch.

Mrs. Dalrymple waved a plump hand at him, proving that she'd been watching them. Encouragement to continue his walk with Miss Mitford?

Or encouragement to leave?

"That might be wise," she said. She seemed to think he'd want to do that right this moment, for she turned with a swirl of her mint-colored skirts and started back up the drive. "Marriage is an important endeavor. Too important to leave to chance."

"I couldn't agree more," he assured her. It was also too important to leave to letters through the mail or one glimpse across a crowded room.

Or even an uncrowded parlor.

True love is all that matters. He heard his mother's voice in his head. *The kind of love that lasts through thick and thin. The kind of love you can build a life around. That's what I want for all my children.*

He wouldn't have admitted it to any of his siblings, but he'd always hoped he might find a love like that. Oh, maybe it would start with a small seed, like the nubs that fell out of the fir cones, but it would grow into a tree that would shelter all those who came upon it.

Could a frontier rancher find that kind of love with a lady from a big city, used to fine things?

His heart seemed to be urging him to find out.

*Learn more at **www.reginascott.com/leftovermob.html**.*

OTHER BOOKS BY REGINA SCOTT

FRONTIER MATCHES
The Perfect Mail-Order Bride
Her Frontier Sweethearts
Frontier Cinderella
The Schoolmarm's Convenient Marriage

FORTUNE'S BRIDES SERIES
Never Doubt a Duke
Never Borrow a Baronet
Never Envy an Earl
Never Vie for a Viscount
Never Kneel to a Knight
Never Marry a Marquess
Always Kiss at Christmas
Never Pursue a Prince
Never Court a Count
Never Romance a Rogue
Never Love a Lord
Never Beguile a Bodyguard
Never Admire an Adventurer
Never Hire a Hero

GRACE-BY-THE-SEA SERIES
The Matchmaker's Rogue
The Heiress's Convenient Husband
The Artist's Healer
The Governess's Earl
The Lady's Second-Chance Suitor
The Siren's Captain

UNCOMMON COURTSHIPS SERIES
The Unflappable Miss Fairchild
The Incomparable Miss Compton
The Irredeemable Miss Renfield
The Unwilling Miss Watkin
An Uncommon Christmas

LADY EMILY CAPERS
Secrets and Sensibilities
Art and Artifice
Ballrooms and Blackmail
Eloquence and Espionage
Love and Larceny

MARVELOUS MUNROES SERIES
My True Love Gave to Me
The Rogue Next Door
The Marquis' Kiss
A Match for Mother

SPY MATCHMAKER SERIES
The Husband Mission
The June Bride Conspiracy
The Heiress Objective

THE REGENT'S DEVICES TRILOGY (writing as
R.E. Scott with Shelley Adina)
The Emperor's Aeronaut
The Prince's Pilot
The Lady's Triumph
The Aeronaut's Heart

And other books from Harper Collins,
Mirror Press, and Revell.

ABOUT THE AUTHOR

REGINA SCOTT STARTED writing novels in the third grade. Thankfully for literature as we know it, she didn't sell her first novel until she learned a bit more about writing. Since her first book was published, her stories have traveled the globe, with translations in many languages, including Dutch, German, Italian, and Portuguese. She now has more than 65 published works of warm, witty romance, and more than one million copies of her books are in reader hands.

While she adores the elegance of the Regency period in England and has penned many stories set then, she loves getting to write about history closer to her home in the Puget Sound area of Washington State, where she lives with her husband. She also loves diving into history headfirst. She has dressed as a Regency dandy, driven four-in-hand, learned to fence, and sailed on a tall ship, all in the name of research, of course. Learn more about her at her website at *www.reginascott.com*.